SAVING VIVIAN

A SECOND CHANCE SECRET BABY ROMANCE.

MICHELLE LOVE

CONTENTS

Made in "The United States" by:

Michelle Love

ISBN: 978-1-64808-813-1

Created with Vellum

BLURBS

I was desperate, sobbing, and already half in love. Why *wouldn't* I accept his proposal?

My whole life I'd been shifting from place to place, looking for one to call home. It was odd that I thought I'd found it after working for Luke Holloway for only three months.

Small wonder that I was drawn to my employer and father of the charge I adored. My entire fantasy was to become Mrs. Luke Holloway and who could blame me—he was rich, gorgeous and available.

What if I got the chance to make that dream my reality?

"He commanded an air of respect, of authority, of unimaginable heat that I felt to my very core." – Vivian Isaac

"But now we were married. I had married the man I had been crushing on since the first week I'd started at the Holloways. And he already regretted it. I could see it on his face." – Vivian Isaac

"He was starting something now that I would be powerless to stop, even if I'd wanted to." – Vivian Isaac

"Slowly, my eyes slid over her form, following the lines of her body—from creamy neck to shapely thighs and up again. Her eyes met mine and we lost a moment simply staring at one another." – Luke Holloway

"She was mine now and I was not going to let her forget it—no matter how loudly she screamed for mercy." – Luke Holloway

"Because there are no men like me. You'll do well to remember that." – Luke Holloway

1

CHAPTER ONE

ivian

I WAS COLDER than I could ever remember being. I shivered violently, staring down at my gloved hands with despair.

How could I be expected to make it out of here alive when my breaths wheezed out in puffs of steam? I knew that lasting even five minutes more was going to be struggle.

Would I survive this weather? Would they find my corpse beneath a pile of melting snow once winter turned to spring?

Only time would tell.

A snowball hit me in the side of my hat-clad head and I whirled around to confront my aggressor.

"How dare you?" I called, my teeth chattering as I spoke. "I'm in survival mode here!"

Lena laughed and reached down into the snow for another ball but I scampered toward the house, claiming mercy.

"Come on, Viv! You're from Canada! You're supposed to be immune to the cold!"

"I'm from Vancouver!" I protested. "This is like Antarctica by comparison!"

Of course, I had never been to Antarctica. But I could only imagine that the cold there was just as unbearable as it was in the outskirts of Boston. I loathed the freezing temperatures, but even I had to admit that there was a stunning beauty to the way the icicles dripped off the pines and created a crystal-like palace of wonderment for my young charge to enjoy.

As long as Lena was happy, I would swallow my deep-seated resentment toward the snow and bask in the warmth of her six-year-old smile.

"Can we please play outside for a couple more minutes?" Lena begged, sensing my desire to run back inside the sprawling ten-thousand-foot mansion to thaw by one of the many fireplaces. "Five more minutes?"

"Five more minutes," I agreed, even though it took every fiber of my being to nod. I felt like I had turned into a block of frozen water, despite the layers of clothes I wore to protect myself.

I would never get used to it, no matter how long I lived in Massachusetts. Like I had explained to Lena a thousand times—my DNA was not set up to combat the cold. Despite being located in the Great White North, Vancouver was mild almost all year round. Sure, we saw snow, but not like this.

"Five minutes," Lena echoed before whipping another snowball at my head. I ducked, but it still hit me, and Lena howled with amusement.

"I'll get you for that one!" I promised with mock anger. "After I can feel my fingers again in three months!"

"I double dog dare you to try!" she chanted back, a wide smile on her sweet, pale face.

She was such a pretty child, was Lena Holloway. If I had ever envisioned one for myself, I would have imagined her to look exactly like the first grader standing in front of me.

Even bundled beneath a wool cap, a scarf tucked snugly about her neck, I could see the wisps of chestnut hair curling around her windblown cheeks. Bright green eyes peered at me mischievously and one dimple touched the middle of her right cheek.

She looks so much like her father, I thought, not for the first time. I was constantly struck by the resemblance between my employer and his only daughter.

Mind you, Luke Holloway and Lena were as different in personality as they could be. True, at Lena's age she was more interested in Christmas stockings than the stock market, but even without the obvious age difference and generational gap, their similarities ended with their good looks.

It was easy to see that Lena would be a social, genial person well into her adult years. Her father was much more brusque and blunt. In short, he was not one to mince words. I guess when you're the CEO of a hedge fund, you don't have a lot of time or patience for niceties.

Not to say he was rude to me, just ... reserved.

"Daddy's home!" Lena called suddenly, and I spun toward the long driveway to see Luke's car heading to the five-car garage around back. The driveway had been salted properly even though the snow had only stopped falling less than an hour earlier. The staff at the Holloway house was more on the ball than any I had ever known. This was my third placement since I'd moved to the States five years earlier, and it was, hands down, my favorite to date.

I idly wondered whether my private thoughts had brought Luke home earlier than normal, and the idea made me blush. I welcomed the heat into my body, the cold all but forgotten.

Slowly, I crunched through the snow after Lena as she ran to greet her father. Luke had stopped his Mercedes halfway up the driveway, and seeing us outside, rolled down the passenger window as we approached.

"Daddy!" Lena yelled. "What are you doing home?"

"Is that any way to greet your old man?" Luke chided, a growl in his voice, but I could see the twinkle in his eye. He adored Lena as much as she did him, and it almost took my breath away to see their close bond.

The last two households I had worked for, both parents had been present but they'd treated their kids like accessories. I certainly hadn't seen anything remotely like the connection that the Holloways seemed to share.

Lena's mother had basically abandoned Lena when she was three, leaving the States to marry a man in Germany. The girl hadn't seen her mother since, a fact that still made my stomach churn every time I thought of it, even after three months of being with them. It was unfathomable to me that a woman could just up and leave her toddler without a second thought. And I wasn't even a mom.

Of course, I'd had many years to ponder such an atrocity, given my own abandonment issues.

Krista, the head of the household staff, had told me about Lena's mom, and while I never brought it up to Luke or Lena, I didn't doubt it was true. There was a deep underlying sadness in Lena, one that I had picked up on almost intuitively—children who had been abandoned by their parents can smell one another out, I think.

At least Lena had Luke. That's better than being a product of the foster care system, I thought. There was no bitterness in the sentiment, just happiness that Lena was cared for. Even after such a short time with the Holloways, I knew I loved that child.

"Sorry, Daddy," Lena chirped with fake seriousness. "Welcome home."

"That's better," he laughed. "Come on, get in the car. I'll drive you back to the house."

It was less than a quarter mile to the house but Lena hurried over the snowbank to spend the extra time with her father.

Luke turned to me, almost as an afterthought, and flashed me a small smile.

"You can come too, Vivian."

I shook my head, feeling the strands of blonde hair caked in ice beneath the collar of my coat.

"I'm fine, Luke, thank you. I'll meet you back at the house."

I wasn't going to interrupt their fleetingly private time together, even if the idea of having the car's heat blasting on my face was the most tempting thing I'd ever known in that instant. I swallowed my desire to jump in after them and instead turned back toward the house.

"Vivian!" Luke called after me, and I glanced over my shoulder. Lena had already buckled herself into the backseat.

"Yes?"

"I have to discuss something with you. Will I see you at dinner? I know it's your night off—"

"No, that's fine," I interjected with too much eagerness. "I have no plans."

Could that have sounded any more pathetic?

I felt like an ass. I could have at least let him finish his sentence before I confessed to my lack of a social life, but I just couldn't seem to keep it together in his presence.

He was just so damned handsome and rich. He commanded an air of respect, of authority, of unimaginable heat that I felt to my very core.

His smile widened slightly and he nodded.

"All right ... are you sure you don't want to get in? You're shivering."

More embarrassment flooded me and I shook my head.

"No, I'm good," I promised. "I'll see you guys inside."

I hurried away before I could humiliate myself further, almost sprinting through the snow, but I eventually forced myself to slow down. The last thing I wanted was to go face-first into a bank while he was still watching me.

Was he still watching me? I hoped so, even though I knew he would only get a glimpse of my thousand pounds of winter clothing.

I had no way of knowing one way or another, but the thought put a smile on my face. When I finally fell in through the front doors, shaking off the ice from my boots, I was still beaming to myself like a moron.

"Did you have fun in the snow?" Krista asked, teasing. She knew how I felt about it. Before I could answer, she looked over my shoulder and out the glass toward the lawn.

"Where's Lena?"

"Luke came home early," I explained, pulling off my outer gear. "She rode up the rest of the way with him."

"Here." Krista reached out and took my gear as I struggled out of it. "You've got mail, by the way."

I glanced toward the massive oak table in the foyer, noticing a small pile of letters on the gleaming surface.

"Thanks."

I ambled toward it, finally rid of my excess clothes, and thanked God for whoever invented heated marble floors. My socks were soaked and I made tracks against the gray and white tiles as I moved.

"I'm going to run upstairs and have a quick bath before dinner," I told her. "Text me if you need anything."

Krista scoffed as if I'd said the most foolish thing she'd ever heard.

"If I need anything? When have you ever known me to need anything?"

"Touché," I agreed, laughing. I turned back toward the twin staircases but she called out to me again.

"Don't forget your mail!"

Grunting, I spun back around and snatched it up, bolting up the steps before she could keep me from the scalding water of my bath for a moment longer.

I SPENT LONGER than I intended warming myself in the tub. When I finally emerged, I looked like a prune.

It was well worth it though, and I took my time dressing for dinner. I knew I was being ridiculous by taking care with my appearance. Logically, I understood that nothing could ever happen between Luke and I, but that didn't stop me from behaving like a girl in the midst of her very first crush.

Anyway, who else was I going to dress up for? It wasn't like I had a bumping social life in Winthrop. There were other nannies that catered to the dozens of wealthy kids in the area, yes, but I more or less kept to myself. I always had.

And there certainly wasn't a line-up of men waiting to date me, that was for sure.

I studied my reflection in the mirror, having settled on a simple but elegant A-line black dress. It accented my honey-blonde hair and made my hazel eyes seem darker, more mysterious somehow. I had a nicely structured face, heart-shaped, they called it, with high cheekbones and long lashes. I wasn't winning any Miss America pageants, but I was nothing to sneeze at.

I'm not bad looking, I thought, turning to check out my ass in the mirror. I had lost all of the baby fat that had plagued me through childhood and my teenage years. And I'd filled out in the right places, even if I did say so myself.

If only I could get Luke to notice that.

Sometimes I wished that I was more like other women my age—bolder, more daring. Unafraid to do what I wanted, when I wanted. I was always so worried about making waves, about doing the right thing. Eighteen years in foster care will teach you a thing or two about conflict and how to avoid it.

I shook my head at my stupid thoughts and moved toward the door. I didn't want to keep the Holloways waiting.

Okay—I didn't want to keep Luke waiting, especially if he had something to discuss with me.

Who knows? I thought with bemusement. *Maybe he's going to declare his undying love for me tonight, in front of everyone.*

I snorted and left my bedroom.

2

CHAPTER TWO

Luke

I FELT the headache coming on even before it happened. It wasn't a migraine or anything, not yet anyway. It was the slow-burning kind, the one that starts at the base of your skull and inches its way up into your brain before you have a fighting chance to stop it.

"Daddy, you look stressed," announced my too-intelligent daughter. "What happened at work today?"

"Nothing that you would be remotely interested in," I assured her. "I didn't sell *Paw Patrol,* if that's what you're asking."

She looked at me with wide, disbelieving eyes.

"You own *Paw Patrol*?" she gasped and I had to laugh. Sometimes I forgot how young she was. Lena had always been an old soul, particularly following her mother's abrupt departure from our lives.

"I don't own *Paw Patrol*," I replied, leaning across the table to cup her small cheek in my hand. "I was just kidding."

She sighed and gave me an exasperated look.

"You can't say things like that to me and then expect me to take you seriously, Daddy."

Again, I was consumed with laughter. Leaving work early was the best thing I could have done for myself. In Lena's company, all the problems of the day seemed miniscule.

Until tomorrow, I thought, my smile faltering slightly.

"Daddy! You're doing that thing with your mouth again!"

Nothing escaped my girl's notice.

"I was just thinking about something," I told her quietly. "I have to go away on business for a few days."

Her eyes bugged and she bolted forward, draping her skinny arms over the sleek wood of the dining table to extend her fingers toward me.

"Daddy! I'm on Christmas vacation! You can't leave at Christmas!"

"Baby, I'm sorry, but it can't be avoided."

A shift in the light caught my attention and I looked up as Vivian entered the room. For a second, I forgot what I was saying as my eyes fell upon her slender, toned frame, perfectly outlined by her dress. Slowly, my eyes slid over her form, following the lines of her body—from creamy neck to shapely thighs and up again. Her eyes met mine and we lost a moment simply staring at one another.

"Hi Viv!" Lena called, breaking the spell between us. "Daddy broke his promise. He's leaving me."

A look of confusion crossed over Vivian's face and she glanced at me, a question in her eyes. I shook my head.

"I'm not breaking my promise and I'm not leaving you," I insisted. "I just need to go out of state for a couple—"

"Leaving me!" Lena interrupted and I scowled at her.

"Lena, mind your manners, please. If you'd let me finish what I have to say—"

"Daddy, you promised no business trips until the new year! It's not the new year and Christmas is next week. What if you don't come back?"

"Is this what you wanted to discuss with me?" Vivian asked, taking her seat next to Lena. I nodded curtly. My attention was on

Lena but I was aware of Vivian's amber-green eyes watching me intently.

"Honey," I started, trying to maintain my patience. "I'm only going to be gone for three days. When I get back, we will do all of our usual Christmas traditions."

Lena pouted and sat back, crossing her arms over her chest. I could see tears of anger forming in her eyes and the guilt was instantaneous.

"We'll be fine, Lena. We can bake cookies and play in the snow—" Vivian started to say in a soothing tone, shooting me a commiserating look.

I had never told the nanny about Kate, Lena's mother, but I got the impression she already knew. How could she not when the entire staff had been with me since before Kate had left? It was human nature to gossip and speculate, so it wasn't a surprise to me that someone might have told her. I suspected that was why Vivian exercised so much calm with Lena, even on the rare occasions when she acted like a brat.

"You hate the snow!" Lena barked in response and I felt my temper flair. Hurt or not, I couldn't tolerate my daughter whining or disrespecting her nanny, not when Vivian gave so much of herself to ensuring that Lena was happy and cared for.

"That's enough! Lena, if you can't behave yourself, you can go to your room."

Shock filled her eyes and she stared at me as if I'd physically struck her. She swallowed visibly and more shame flooded me, but before I could say anything to diffuse the situation, she leapt from the table and ran from the dining room, leaving Vivian and I to stare after her.

"Shit," I muttered. "I could have handled that better."

"She'll be all right," Vivian reassured me. She rose to follow after Lena but I stopped her.

"She's got abandonment issues," I heard myself say, and Vivian looked at me in surprise. She didn't speak but she did nod slowly, the look in her eyes telling me that I was right to suspect that she'd already known.

"It's impossible to juggle everything sometimes."

I had no idea why I was unloading on the nanny. She didn't get paid enough to listen to my personal problems, but the stress of everything that was happening at work was coming to a peak, and I couldn't keep it bottled up anymore.

Sadly, Vivian was on the receiving end of it.

"That's why you have help, Luke." She didn't seem put off in the least by my uncharacteristic outburst. "It takes a village to raise a child."

"I did promise her not to take any business trips around Christmas," I continued. "She's not wrong to be mad."

"Well, why don't you take her with you?"

My head whipped up and I stared at her through narrowed eyes.

"I can't take her with me—I've got back-to-back meetings ..."

Our gazes locked and she grinned.

"But if you come with us," I finished, reading her thoughts. I frowned as soon as the words left my lips. "But you're due this weekend off. I don't want to ask you to give up your time off to come with me. I mean, I'll pay extra, of course, but ..."

"I would be working anyway," she reminded me quickly. "If I had to stay here. What difference does it make?"

I realized she had a point, although it only made me feel worse about having to put her in this situation at all. I shoved that aside. She was my employee—why would I feel bad about making her work a little overtime? It wasn't like I didn't pay her well. She had her own suite and I gave her regular days off. Vivian had certainly never complained, and she genuinely seemed to enjoy being with Lena. I'd sometimes watch the two together and be consumed with this combination of pride and fury when I saw how my daughter interacted with her nanny.

Kate never showed Lena an iota of the attention that the nanny does.

I knew I was lucky to have Vivian. There had been two previous nannies before her—both of them a bad match. One had sued me for wrongful dismissal when I found out she'd been turning tricks in her bedroom while Lena was napping.

Yeah, I was happy that Vivian was with us.

But as I nodded at her, slowly firming up the plans to add them to the flight the following morning, I found my eyes wandering down the firm curve of her breasts and along the flat stomach beneath her dress. I couldn't help myself—I was a red-blooded male, after all, and she ... well, she was all woman, even if she tried not to call attention to herself.

Could it be that the reason I felt guilty about asking her to come with us was because it felt too much like I was propositioning her?

Are you crazy? I snapped at myself. *Even if your mind was going there, nothing could ever happen between you and the nanny. Your life is complicated enough without throwing in a sordid affair with a member of your household staff.*

"Three days?" Vivian asked, halting my runaway thoughts. "That's what I should pack for?"

I bobbed my head, wrenching myself back into the present. I forced any thoughts that were not business and/or Lena-related out of my mind, because God knew I had enough on my plate without adding fantasies of undressing the nanny to the mix.

"Make it four, just in case," I replied slowly. "Pack a swimsuit. There are two pools at the hotel."

I was going to have to arrange for another suite for Lena and Vivian. I knew that my schedule was going to keep me out at all hours of the night entertaining prospective investors, so I'd need my own space.

"Lena will love that," Vivian offered, rising from her chair. "I'll let her know the good news."

"No, no," I told her, picking up my napkin from where I had draped it over my lap. "I'll tell her. I'm the one who needs the brownie points, not you."

She laughed and reclaimed her chair.

"True."

I sauntered toward the entranceway of the house, pausing to look up toward the second-floor interior balcony, half-expecting to see Lena sitting there, eavesdropping. It wouldn't have been the first time I'd caught her there, but it seemed that she was really upset this time and had retreated to her room to cry.

"Oh ..." I heard Vivian sigh and I looked back at her.

"What's wrong?"

"I just realized that my passport needs renewing," she grunted. "Please tell me your business is in the States?"

"No fear there. It is. Actually ..." I smiled. "You'll be happy to know that we'll be getting far away from the snow you apparently hate."

I watched her cheeks turn pink.

"I don't hate the snow," she mumbled, but even I knew she was lying.

"Well, in any case, we're going to the desert."

She blinked at me, almost uncomprehendingly.

"The desert?" she echoed, and I realized it sounded less disturbing saying it in my head. I quickly finished my thought.

"Yes. We're going to Las Vegas."

3

CHAPTER THREE

ivian

NOT ONLY HAD I never been to Vegas, I'd never had a desire to go. I had never been one to gamble, not really. Sure, I'd thrown a quarter in a slot machine back home when I'd gotten dragged to the casino with my friends, and I'd played a hand or two of poker, but visiting Sin City? Not really my thing.

However, when Luke's private jet landed on the airstrip on Thursday afternoon, my feelings toward the infamous city almost immediately changed.

It wasn't hot like I had expected it to be, but compared to the coast, it was damned balmy. I would take fifty-nine degrees to thirty-five any day of the week.

Lena, like I, was in awe of the touristy display of the Vegas strip as we made our way to a hotel I'd never heard of. We traveled in style in a Hummer limousine that Luke had rented.

It seemed like overkill to me but I'd never been on a business trip with him before. For all I knew, this was how he rode all the time.

But a part of me wondered if he hadn't done it up on purpose.

You really are delusional, I told myself, shaking my head.

Luke caught my look and snickered. "It's ostentatious, isn't it?"

Worried that my thoughts were apparent on my face, I gaped at him in embarrassment.

"No ... no, it's great," I told him lamely. "It's bigger than I expected."

He frowned slightly, though there was still an amused look in his green eyes.

"Funny. I thought Vegas was a lot smaller than I'd expected the first time I saw it."

I understood then that he wasn't talking about the limo. I didn't really know how to respond.

"Daddy, can we go to all those places with the lights?" Lena asked, whirling around from the window to look at us. I knew she had no idea what took place inside the flashy buildings.

"I found a lot of things for us to do while your dad is working," I assured her. "There's a circus, an amusement park—"

"With rides?" Lena squealed and I nodded. Her face was alight with excitement. I noticed the grateful look Luke gave me and felt a spark of satisfaction. Of course, I would have made all the arrangements, regardless, but knowing that he was happy about my choices made me feel ... I don't know. Useful?

Was that my plan? To become indispensable to him? I'd had worse plans in the past.

I cleared my throat, feeling a little embarrassed by my self-reflective thoughts, and turned my eyes back out the tinted windows. I wished then that I'd taken Luke up on his offer to have a drink when we'd first gotten into the limo.

This is not a date, Vivian. You're working.

Why was I having such a hard time remembering all of a sudden?

We pulled up to a gated entranceway, which was not unlike the one surrounding the Holloway house. The driver stopped to speak into the intercom before the wrought iron gave way and permitted us through.

"A gated hotel?" I asked, half in awe, half alarmed. I'd never seen anything like this. I hadn't even known they existed.

"Wait until you see the inside," Luke told us. "It's spectacular."

I didn't doubt it, particularly when our car was met by three bellhops outside a boutique-style entranceway flanked in a marble archway.

"Welcome to the Reverie, Mr. Holloway," a fourth person announced, appearing seemingly from thin air. She was a slight thing, maybe five-foot-four, but with an air of dignity and old money, despite her seemingly young age.

"Hi Cammy. This is my daughter Lena and her nanny, Vivian Isaac."

Cammy blatantly ignored me, literally turning her back toward me to crouch down and make the fakest cooing noises to Lena.

"Oh, aren't you a darling!" she squealed. "Your daddy talks about you all the time."

Lena stared up at her with calculating emerald eyes as she studied her face.

"He's never talked about you," my little hero countered. It took every ounce of willpower I had not to high-five Lena for that comment.

Cammy lost her phony smile and abruptly spun on her heel, clicking toward the entrance, suddenly losing interest in kissing Luke's ass through his daughter.

I swallowed a grin and followed after Luke and Lena, casting a final look around the front of the hotel. I spent a moment taking in the onyx fountains and hand-painted stone around the exotic flowers embracing a granite sign that I hadn't noticed upon entry.

The Reverie, indeed, I thought, making my way inside the open-plan lobby. It was more of an atrium, the levels leading up all visible from the ground floor and embraced in glass. It felt futuristic and, I admit, a little scary.

"I have you in your usual suite, Mr. Holloway, and I've put Miss Holloway in the adjoining suite with the help," Cammy said crisply, handing Luke two fobs. She still hadn't looked at me, but she didn't have to for me to feel the resentment radiating off of her and toward me.

"Miss Isaac is my daughter's nanny," Luke snapped, and my head jerked around at his tone. He sounded furious, though I couldn't understand why.

"I know that, Mr. Holloway. You've already explained that."

"Did I, at any time, introduce her as 'the help' or 'my help' or use the word 'help' whatsoever?"

My lips parted in surprise as I watched his infamous temper flaring. Shivers erupted over my body at his fierceness.

He was defending my honor ... kind of.

"I didn't mean anything by it," Cammy muttered, looking as shocked as I felt. I had barely heard the jibe, but honestly, I was used to being looked at as a lower-class citizen among my wealthy employers. It didn't bother me ... well, it didn't bother me much.

"Can you kindly rephrase what you just said?" It wasn't a question, it was a command, and Cammy wasted no time fixing her faux pas.

"I have put Miss Holloway and Miss Isaac in the suite adjacent to yours, Mr. Holloway."

"That's better."

He spun, grabbing Lena by the hand. I couldn't stop myself from looking at Cammy, who returned my almost apologetic gaze balefully. I knew it wasn't my fault that she'd just gotten a verbal dressing-down, but I felt mildly responsible for the encounter. Cammy, on the other hand, seemed to think I was fully responsible.

I turned away, hurrying after father and daughter. Luke was still glowering when we got into the elevator and I wasn't sure if I should say anything or not. Thankfully, my little savior piped up on my behalf.

"Why were you so mad at that lady, Daddy?"

Luke cast me a sidelong glance.

"Because some people are rude, honey, and need to be put in their place."

"Who was she rude to?" Lena asked, and a hot flush filled my face. He really was making a bigger deal out of it than he needed to, but he was my boss and I didn't want to contradict him in front of Lena.

Or maybe you're just secretly pleased.

"It doesn't matter, Lena. You just always remember to be kind, okay? You're no better than anyone else in this world just because you're lucky enough to have money."

Lena's head cocked backward to look up at her father's face with interest.

"I have money?"

"Never mind," Luke sighed, realizing that his life lesson had been lost on his young daughter.

The elevator stopped on the nineteenth floor. There was only one floor higher, and I guessed it housed one of the pools and a restaurant.

"This way, Mr. Holloway," the bellhop instructed, struggling with the bag I'd packed for both Lena and me. We stopped before one of the penthouse suites and I looked around in confusion. There were only two suites on the floor. If he had one and we had the adjoining ...

"Ladies, you are across the hall," another bellhop called to us.

Oh. We had our own penthouse too.

Ostentatious indeed.

"Why don't you two get freshened up and we'll meet for a late lunch," Luke suggested. "I've got to make some phone calls, but I'll knock on your door when I'm done."

"Can I stay with you, Daddy?" Lena asked.

"Why don't you help me pick out what to wear, Lena?" I told her, knowing that Luke had to refuse her request. He couldn't work with her chirping in the background.

For a minute, I thought Lena might refuse, but she nodded, albeit grudgingly, and took my extended hand. Luke shot me a grateful look and we exchanged a small smile.

"Give me an hour, tops," he promised.

"Take your time," I replied nonchalantly. "Ladies need time to look our best, don't we, Lena?"

"It's true, Daddy. Princesses can't get ready in ten minutes."

I gave Luke a meaningful look and he lost the expression of annoyance he'd been carrying since leaving the front desk.

"Noted," he replied dryly.

I used the fob to unlock the door and gasped in awe at the pretty apartment spread before us.

It had all the comforts of home, including a state-of-the-art kitchen, two fireplaces, and a sunken living room.

The wraparound balcony overlooked the city in all its splendor. It made me a little nervous, the clear glass seeming like too small a barrier.

"I like the one in Paris better," my princess ward informed me, and I had to giggle. At her age, I had been living in my fourth foster home in a basement bedroom with two other kids.

I joined her in the master bedroom, where Lena had managed to open the suitcase. The bellhop had offered to send up a maid to put everything away but I'd refused. There was only so much pampering I could permit before my head exploded.

"Can we go swimming?" Lena asked me eagerly and I nodded.

"We have three days here," I reminded her. "Let's pace ourselves."

Lena pouted but then flopped on the edge of the bed, swinging her legs lightly.

"Are you and my dad boyfriend and girlfriend?"

The bluntness of the question both threw me and embarrassed me.

"I ... what? How do you know about boyfriends?" I demanded, settling on the best deflection I could muster under the pressure.

"You didn't answer my question."

Maybe she was more like her father than I realized. She would make a hell of a CEO in her own right someday.

"No, of course not!" I replied. "Where would you ever get that idea?"

I hoped she wouldn't notice how deep of a red my cheeks had become. Lena didn't answer right away and I stopped pretending to fuss with my clothes to look at her.

"Lena?"

Her face looked unbearably sad, and I felt a twinge of worry.

"I was just hoping," she finally answered meekly. "I like you better than any of my other nannies. I like you better than my mom."

A pang of alarm and hurt touched my soul. I reached toward her, brushing a stray strand of dark hair out of her crestfallen face.

"I like you too," I told her softly. "No matter what happens, I will always like you, okay?"

She peered at me. "But if you and Daddy were boyfriend and girlfriend, you would be like my mom, wouldn't you?"

"Honey, I don't need to be with your dad to care about you," I said, a lump forming in my throat.

"I guess."

It was not the answer she wanted to hear, but what else could I tell her?

Sorry, kid, but men like your dad don't fall for the help. That only happens in fairy tales. That would never do.

"Come on," I urged her, determined to erase the stricken look from her face. "You're supposed to help me dress, remember?"

She nodded but I could see her heart wasn't into it.

"What about this one?" I asked teasingly, pulling out my full-piece bathing suit. "Is this appropriate for lunch?"

To my relief, she giggled and reached into the suitcase herself.

"Only if you wear it with this skirt."

As she pulled out the garment, a letter fell to the ground. I peered at it with interest as Lena slid off the bed to retrieve it.

"What's that?" she asked, handing it to me. I realized it was the mail I'd picked up the previous day on my way up to my bath. I must have slipped it into my suitcase in my rush to pack. I barely had a chance to glance at the letterhead when there was a knock at the adjoining door.

"Daddy's done already!" Lena screeched with excitement, running toward the door, which met at the kitchen.

I tossed the envelope onto the bed and rushed over to meet them, but when I got to where Luke stood framed by the door, I could see something was wrong.

"I can't do lunch," he said grimly and without preamble. "Something came up."

He handed me a credit card and nodded toward Lena.

"I have no idea what time I'll be back, but put anything you need to on that card and keep your cell on. I'll call you if I get out of this early."

Something in his tone told me he had absolutely no faith in that happening.

"Daddy, you promised!" Lena grunted in frustration.

"Just go," I mouthed to Luke. I could tell a meltdown was imminent, and I knew I couldn't let Luke bear the brunt of it. It was obvious that his stress levels were mounting.

He crouched down to hug his daughter.

"Be good for Vivian," he said tiredly. I couldn't help but feel bad for him. Whatever was happening at work was taking its toll on him.

"But Daddy—"

"Last one in the pool has to help Krista with Christmas dinner dishes," I chimed in, subtly gesturing for Luke to go.

Lena spun and glared at me, but I could see the mention of the pool had already distracted her.

"No fair!" she complained. "You have longer legs! You'll get there faster!"

Life isn't fair, kid, I thought silently. *If it was, I might actually have a shot at being your dad's girlfriend, not just "the help."*

4

CHAPTER FOUR

Luke

I FREELY ADMITTED that I was drunk, and I was apologizing to no one for that. After the night I'd had, meeting with my partner and discussing our options for a merger or sale in the future, I just wanted to drown my sorrows and forget the night had ever happened.

It was our last night in Vegas, after what had been a blur of meetings and dinners, and one particularly terrible show with some popular R&B artist whose voice reminded me of a cat in heat.

The entire purpose of the visit had been to secure our investors, some of whom had grown leery following a particularly bad month in the stock market. Dozens of variables had contributed to a series of bad ventures and the company I had single-handedly built was looking at its first real scare in fifteen years.

It was Dave who had suggested Vegas, and I had been against the idea initially. I'd never really been a fan of the flashy city, but my colleague Dave Kutchings knew PR and I couldn't exactly brush him off when his idea was solid. No matter how much I loathed the idea of wining and dining the most obnoxious men and women imaginable in the most offensive place on earth.

Moreover, I was mildly disgusted with myself for having brought my six-year-old to Vegas, although it had seemed like a good idea at the time.

It doesn't matter now. The crisis is averted—for now—and we return to Boston tomorrow.

I had not seen Lena once since that first day, and to say I felt guilty was an understatement. I was wracked with self-loathing because I had purposely avoided her and Vivian, knowing that I'd be met with a temper tantrum. Of course, I'd spoken to Vivian, who assured me that they were having a great time. But I know she could be trying to placate me. If Lena was miserable, she wouldn't be eager to tell me, I was sure. That's what I paid her the big bucks for, after all.

I reminded myself to give Vivian a huge Christmas bonus.

My commitments had been more time-consuming than I'd initially imagined, and the past two nights I'd arrived back to my suite after three a.m. My intention had been to sneak into the girls' suite and check on Lena, but I didn't want to scare Vivian when I was sure she was asleep.

That night, however, it was just after midnight and I missed my child. I wanted to at least give her a kiss for the first time in days, and like I said—I was feeling no pain. The shots at Caesar's Palace were warming my stomach and clouding my judgement just enough that I walked through the adjoining door between our suites without so much as a second thought.

The lights were mostly on and I exhaled with relief. At least Vivian was still awake—or at least it looked like she was.

"Vivian?" I called in a stage whisper. "Are you here?"

It was a dumb question—where else would she be?

I closed the door behind me and crept inside the suite, suddenly feeling ridiculous. In a moment of clarity, I stood in the kitchenette, debating whether to leave, but I knew Lena was only a few feet away. I would just give her a kiss and—

A noise distracted me from finishing my own thought and I tensed, listening.

"Vivian?" I called again, my voice low. I moved toward the sunken living room and that was when I saw her, curled up on the couch, tears streaking her face.

"Oh shit," I muttered, rushing toward her. "What happened? Where's Lena?"

She jerked her head up and stared at me in shock. She obviously hadn't heard me come in. I noticed the empty bottle of pinot grigio on the coffee table and a spark of anger slid through me.

"Are you drunk?" I demanded, realizing with embarrassment that I was slurring my own words.

But *you're not the one being paid to care for your daughter.*

Hastily, she wiped the tears from her face and shook her head.

"No, Luke," she muttered, turning her head like she didn't want me to see her bloodshot eyes. "I've been working on that bottle since the first day."

I instantly relaxed. She didn't seem inebriated—just really upset. I moved closer to her side and perched beside her on the couch, my eyebrows raising to stare at her questioningly.

"Why are you crying? Is it Lena?"

"No, of course not." There was almost annoyance in her voice. "I would have told you if something was wrong with Lena."

I reasoned that she was right and I shook my head, trying to muster some clarity on the situation. It was then that I saw the letter lying on the coffee table, next to the empty bottle.

Without asking her permission, I reached forward to grab it.

"No, wait!" Vivian gasped, reaching for my hand, but it was too late. I saw exactly what it read and blood began to rush to my head.

"What is this?" I demanded, waving it around, my voice raising. "How long have you known about this?"

"I just found out," she muttered. "When we got here. I was going to tell you when we got home."

I scoffed and reread the impersonal letter that was going to ruin my daughter's life.

"How could you let this happen?" I snapped at her. "Why didn't you say anything to me?"

"They changed the laws, Luke! I had no idea that it was this bad, especially as a Canadian citizen, but ..."

She trailed off and nodded toward the letter from the United States Citizenship and Immigration Services.

"I'll have my lawyers get on this," I huffed. "You're not going anywhere."

"There's no time," she moaned. "I need to be back in Vancouver by next week or they'll come for me."

"I won't let them!" I said insistently, but even as I said it, I thought about how even a minor scandal like this would affect my company. I couldn't afford to be mixed up in harboring an illegal worker, not with the political climate being how it was.

What a fucking mess.

"I have to go home," Vivian said softly, a fresh bout of tears flooding her shining hazel eyes. "I don't have a choice, Luke."

There was no way I was letting her go, not when Lena had bonded with her better than anyone since her wretched mother had disappeared. My daughter would never recover from such a blow.

"No," I insisted. "You're not going anywhere. Let me make some phone calls and—"

"You can't get caught up in this."

She said it with such gentle finality that it left me stunned.

"I know your company has been having problems," she muttered, shifting her gaze away from me. "The last thing you need is one more."

"And what do you think will happen when Lena finds out you're leaving?" I demanded. "You think that won't cause a bit of friction?"

I didn't mean for it to come out sounding so sarcastically, but my emotions were on overdrive. And seeing the torment in her face was not helping matters. My mind raced, considering our options.

"I'm calling my attorney right now."

She didn't stop me as I pulled out my phone and fumbled for Cory Stephen's number in my contacts, but I didn't see a lot of hope in her eyes.

My attorney answered on the fourth ring, and he sounded pissed off.

"Not business hours," he muttered at me.

"It's ten o'clock where you are," I snapped back. "Who goes to bed at ten o'clock?"

"A father of four," he countered. "What is it, Luke?"

"I have a problem and it's urgent."

My confession prompted a deep sigh on the other end of the phone, but I continued on. I explained to him that my nanny was about to be sent home on an expired visa.

"So? File the paperwork and bring her back. It shouldn't take more than a few months."

I thought of how much Lena would change in a few months, how the trust she had built not only with Vivian but with me would fade.

No. She's been through too much already. I'm not letting my daughter be abandoned again, even temporarily.

"She's not leaving, not for a day," I told him. "Give me another solution."

I felt Vivian watching me through her peripheral vision, but there was no expectation on her face. I could see she didn't have any faith in my ability to keep her with us.

"Luke, you're already knee deep in toxic waste," Cory reminded me. "Just go through the proper channels before your investors—"

"I didn't ask for a business lesson," I growled. "Give me a solution."

There was a long silence before my lawyer spoke again. When he did speak, the hairs on my arms rose in anticipation and my eyes darted toward Vivian. She had laid her head back against the couch and closed her eyes.

"I see," I mumbled, my head swimming after he had finished. "And this will work?"

"I don't recommend it, Luke. You'll have the government on your ass—"

"Thanks, Cory."

I disconnected the call, not wanting to hear anymore of his warnings. He didn't need to spell out the trouble that would lie ahead if I went through with it, but I thought of the alternative. Lena would be torn apart if I didn't do it.

It's the only way.

"He can't help," Vivian said dully.

"He helped," I replied slowly, tossing my cell onto the coffee table. "There's a way that you can stay, but you might not like it."

She looked at me expectantly, confusion twisting her lovely face.

"What is it?"

"You can marry me."

The statement hung in the air like stale cigarette smoke and I tried to decipher the expression on her face. I don't think I'd seen anything like it in my life. It was a combination of surprise and disbelief, coupled with ... desire?

"It's asking a lot of you," I continued before she could refuse. "But, of course, it wouldn't be a real marriage, and as soon as your citizenship comes through, I'll give you a divorce."

Her face twisted some more, and I felt like I was saying the wrong thing.

"A divorce?" she mumbled. "What about Lena?"

My heart skipped a beat. A divorce would not fare well with her either. But if Vivian stayed in the house, even after we split, it would be a non-issue, wouldn't it? Anyway, we could deal with that when the time came.

I said as much aloud.

"Let's deal with one problem at a time," I replied smoothly. "This is the more pressing issue, Vivian. We're already in Vegas. It will be easy to find someone to marry us tonight. That will move the paperwork along, according to Cory."

Her face screwed up in what I could only assume was consternation, and I knew I was putting a lot of pressure on her. But it was our last night in Vegas ...

"Vivian, I know it's—"

"Yes," she interrupted quickly, and it was my turn to be confused.

"Yes, it's a lot to ask?"

She shook her head, a tentative smile forming on her lips.

"No. Yes, I'll marry you."

5

CHAPTER FIVE

ivian

Both Luke and I were silent on the flight home, trying to process what we'd done the night before.

Did he regret how we'd called the all-night babysitting service to watch Lena while we found the closest wedding chapel and made our illegal activities official?

Did he resent me for agreeing to marry him when he obviously wasn't thinking clearly?

What was going to happen once we got home and USCIS came knocking on the door?

For my part, I didn't know how I felt about it.

Okay, that's a lie—I was ecstatic. I was Mrs. Luke Holloway, if only in name. I was now technically Lena's stepmom, a fact we had yet to disclose to her.

I cast him a furtive look but he seemed glued to whatever had captured his attention on his tablet.

"DADDY!" Lena hollered. "Are you even listening to me?"

"Yes." His tone was flat and that was enough to deflate my excitement like a pinpricked balloon. He sounded defeated and unhappy.

"What did I say then?" Lena challenged, folding her arms over her chest and staring at him defiantly.

"You were telling me about all the places you saw in Vegas."

Again, there was no emotion in his voice, no indication that he felt anything other than regret about his decision from the previous night.

Oh God. What had we done? How would Lena react when we told her?

It wasn't something we'd discussed, but sooner or later it would have to be dealt with.

"Daddy, I haven't seen you in three whole days," Lena complained. "Can't you pretend to pay attention to me now?"

A stab of sadness touched my heart. Lena wasn't trying to be a brat. I knew she had missed Luke during our stay in Sin City. Even though I'd done my best to distract and exhaust her so she would fall asleep as soon as we returned to the hotel, clearly something had been missing for her during the trip.

Staying focused on Lena hadn't been an easy task, considering I had opened the letter that very first day and been sitting on a ball of frustration and worry ever since. I had planned to tell Luke about it when we returned to Boston, but obviously he had found out first. If I'd known he was going to come to our suite that night, then I would have hidden the letter—and maybe put on something more provocative than a set of monkey pajamas.

But now we were married. I had married the man I had been crushing on since the first week I'd started working for the Holloways.

And he already regretted it. I could see it on his face.

"I'm not ignoring you, Lena," Luke sighed, setting his tablet aside. "I'm just very tired. I didn't get much sleep last night."

For the first time since boarding the private plane, Luke glanced at me, a wry smile forming on his lips. My heart skipped and a deep sense of relief washed over me as I realized that he didn't hate me—or at least not as much as I thought he did.

"Why not?" Lena asked curiously. "Were you in meetings?"

He chuckled softly and gestured for her to climb into his lap. Eagerly, Lena jumped from her seat and leapt onto his lap, laying her head against his chest. My chest swelled with that familiar feeling I got whenever I saw the closeness between them. But this time it was coupled with envy, wishing I could be the one on Luke's lap. I wanted to be the one hearing his heartbeat against my ear, inhaling the scent of his sporty aftershave, being comforted by him.

Maybe one day ...

I forced myself not to let my mind go there. Ours was not a union based on feelings for anyone other than Lena. Neither one of us wanted her to suffer anymore than she already had, and we'd done what we had to do to make sure that didn't happen.

That's why we're committing a crime against the United States government—to ensure her happiness.

"No, I didn't have late meetings," Luke told her. "I actually came to see you when I was finished last night but you were already asleep."

Lena moved her head back to study his face.

"You did?" she demanded. "Why didn't you wake me up?"

"Because you were sleeping like an angel and I knew I would see you today."

She looked at me, her eyes suspicious.

"It's true," I conceded. "He did."

"Lena," Luke continued, shooting me a quick look before turning his gaze back to the girl. "Vivian and I have something to talk to you about."

My face paled and I opened my mouth to protest.

He couldn't tell her now! We had no idea how she would react.

I thought about the discussion Lena and I had had on the first day, the one where she had asked if I was her dad's girlfriend.

She might think we've been lying to her or—

"Vivian and I got married last night."

Well. So much for thinking it through.

Lena gasped and her eyes bugged.

"What?" she choked. "You got married? How? When? Are you lying?"

She looked at me and I tried to read her expression, but the surprise overrode anything else she might be feeling.

"No," Luke told her kindly, still stroking her long, dark curls. "Vivian is your stepmother now."

Lena's head whipped around to look at me and dread knotted in my stomach as I waited for the accusations to start flying. Oh, how I wished that Luke hadn't said anything without talking to me first—but then again, why should he? I was still his employee, technically. He didn't need my say-so to do anything. Even if he was my husband now, too.

Before I could formulate words of comfort for Lena, she propelled herself off her father's lap and into mine, sending my pod chair spinning as she squealed.

"I knew it!" she howled happily. "I knew you and Daddy were a thing!"

"A thing?" Luke and I echoed in unison. Where did she pick this stuff up from?

"Are you okay with this?" I asked her but I knew I already had my answer.

"Yeah!"

I relaxed and relished the feel of her small body pressed into mine. I permitted myself one more look at Luke and I instantly recognized the look on his face—it was the same one I wore when I saw him with Lena.

I sighed quietly and sat back, pulling Lena closer to me. Maybe we hadn't done such a bad thing after all.

If Lena handled the news of our marriage well, the house staff did not. I couldn't fault them for talking about me behind my back, but I admit that it hurt that Krista, whom I had considered my friend, suddenly looked at me like I was some gold-digging bitch. I wanted to tell her the truth but Luke had been very clear about the rules of our marriage.

"No one can ever know the real reason we got married. When USCIS comes, there cannot be a single flaw in our story. You came here, we fell in love, we decided to get married in Vegas. That's it. There's nothing else to tell. If anyone learns the truth, it could weaken our case."

I knew he was right but it didn't stop me from feeling apprehensive about the looks that the employees gave me.

There was a heaviness in the air as Lena and I decorated the house for Christmas, even though she was in good spirits.

"I can't wait to get back to school and tell everyone I have a new mom!" she chortled. The words filled me with both pride and worry. One day, she would have to tell those very same friends that her dad and new mom had split.

Unless Luke learns to love me ...

I quieted that wily voice in my head. I couldn't deny that those thoughts were popping up more and more frequently though.

"Where should we put this garland?" Lena chirped, and we looked for a place to set it. The entire mansion looked like Santa had thrown up in it. There was not a single hallway or common area that wasn't littered in green or red and tinsel. There were four real Christmas trees, all adorned to the point where the needles were almost completely covered.

I couldn't imagine how much money had been spent on decorations over the years. Probably more than my yearly salary.

"I've gotta get some more tinsel," Lena announced suddenly and I laughed.

"Honey, I don't think there is anymore."

"I'm going to the city," Krista declared, stalking into the living room, and I bristled instinctively. I wondered if she had been spying on us.

Paranoid much?

It was hard not to be when I knew I was doing something so

wrong, and keeping it a secret from everyone. The girl who never made waves was suddenly on the wrong side of a huge secret, and I really didn't like the way this shoe fit.

"Do you want to keep me company, Lena?" Krista continued, easing my suspicion a little bit. I realized the housekeeper had only come looking for Lena.

Lena looked at me.

"Do you want to go to the city?"

I had Christmas presents to wrap and I could use the opportunity to do it without Lena catching me. I glanced at Krista.

"I have some things to take care of here," I told her. "Will you guys be okay by yourselves?"

Krista snorted contemptuously. "We got along just fine before you got here, *Mrs. Holloway*. I think we'll manage."

Her clipped tone sent a shiver of anxiety through me but I managed a smile.

"Great."

I turned to Lena and ruffled her hair playfully.

"Have fun. I'll see you at dinner, okay?"

She nodded and they turned toward the door, leaving me alone in the foyer covered in glitter.

I wished the knot of uncertainty in my stomach would dissolve, but I knew it would take a Christmas miracle for that to happen overnight.

It's only been two days. It will get better.

"You look like you should be on top of a Christmas tree," Luke commented, coming up behind me. I turned and laughed.

"I'll take that as a compliment," I replied. "But it's hard not to be covered in sparkles in this house. What is this?"

He smiled ruefully, closing the short space between us. I was taken aback at his nearness, but my body responded instantly. To add to my surprise, he reached up to pull a strand of tinsel from my bun. I blushed and looked down.

"I try to make Christmas really special for Lena," he explained. "She loves it, as all kids do, and it's easy to indulge her on this."

"It's hard not to be infected by the season," I agreed and Luke snorted.

"Not a fan of Christmas?"

"Never really had one," I replied before I could stop myself. Luke studied my face, his brow furrowing.

"You don't celebrate Christmas?"

I shrugged, trying to seem nonchalant. "I've never really celebrated anything. I grew up ..." I had to stop and catch my breath, although I couldn't say why it troubled me to speak about it. I had come to terms with my upbringing, my lack of family or ties. Why was it so difficult to talk about?

"You grew up poor?" Luke guessed gently. "It's nothing to be ashamed of, Viv."

He'd called me "Viv." Like we were more than just an employee and her employer.

"Well, yes," I laughed nervously. "But also in foster care. If I happened to be with a family who celebrated anything at all, it was hardly memorable. I remember hating being taken out of school for Christmas breaks. Since I've been out of the system on my own, I usually go see a movie on Christmas Day or order Chinese food. It's always just been another day to me."

Luke's face showed his surprise at my story, and I was a little startled to see that. I would have thought that he'd done a thorough background check on me. But I had come recommended to him through the last family for whom I'd worked, so maybe he hadn't bothered.

"I'm sorry," he said gruffly. "I didn't realize. If this is too much for you, Vivian, you can ..."

He stopped himself from speaking, as if he realized what he was about to say. What could I do? Sit Christmas out? Take a few days off? That was hardly an option, not with the way everything had changed.

Anyway, I had no desire to do that, not when I was genuinely getting into the spirit, thanks to Lena.

I shook my head to let him off the hook and smiled warmly.

"I wouldn't dream of it," I replied truthfully. "I'm getting in the mood for the first time since I can remember. I think it will be different this year."

The look in Luke's eyes was different than anything I'd ever seen from him. It was as if there was a light glimmering behind his blazing emerald eyes, making his irises look ethereal. He still stood just inches from me, and my heart jumped.

He's looking at me like a woman for once, I thought, my pulse quickening. *Not just his daughter's nanny.*

"Your Christmases are going to be much different from now on," he told me gruffly. "You'll see."

My breaths became uneven as he moved his face toward me, brushing his lips softly against mine. My knees were ready to buckle but I steeled myself against falling. I was afraid to move, lest I break whatever spells had come over him.

My eyes closed and I inhaled his scent deeply into my lungs, my head growing heady with a sense of elation I'd never known.

Could this really be happening? It was all I'd wanted for so long —for Luke to see me as something more than his employee. It looked like my dreams were finally coming true.

Don't pinch yourself. You'll wake up.

But there was nothing fake about his kiss or the way his arm looped around my waist, pulling me toward him so I could feel the lines of his solid frame against mine. I trembled slightly, my mouth parting. Our tongues instantly connected, sending a spark of electricity all the way through to my toes.

He was everything I'd dreamed he'd be, his lips soft and exploring, his hands strong, grasping me securely. I felt myself melt against him, knowing that if I'd ever had any resolve, it was long gone.

Luke's lips trailed down along my chin and across my throat, his palms splaying across my butt cheeks and drawing me closer. Instantly, I felt the bulge of his excitement against my belly and my heart beat so fast I worried I might black out.

But he seemed to sense my propensity for swooning and, without warning, scooped me up in his arms. I stared into his eyes in stunned silence, knowing that he fully intended to see this act through.

I'd been wanting this for so long, but I had no idea he'd want this too.

He wasn't drunk or worried about his daughter. He wanted me like a man wanted a woman, and I could hardly believe it was happening.

"Let's consummate this marriage," he told me. Goosebumps exploded all over my skin.

I nodded but his mouth had already latched back onto my neck. He started walking and I felt like I was floating on a magic carpet; he continued to the stairs, climbing with me lying helplessly in his arms.

He was starting something now that I would be powerless to stop, even if I had wanted to.

6

CHAPTER SIX

Luke

SOMETHING HAD TAKEN OVER ME, counteracting my common sense. Maybe it was the plaintive way she looked at me, or the way my gut reacted when I learned she had been an abandoned child too.

Whatever the reason, I couldn't stop myself from mounting the stairs, my mouth secured on her soft throat, my body yearning to possess her in a way I'd never felt before.

We were in my suite before I knew it, Vivian sprawled out over the black and white bedspread of my California king bed. I didn't remember taking off her clothes, but when I sat back to look at her, she was naked, her lithe body demanding my full attention.

I could read the look of hopeful bemusement on her face but I didn't want to think about what this could mean for us.

She was quivering, and the realization only fueled my desire to have her. I didn't waste another second staring into her face. I was driven by something primal. Feral.

My mouth moved over the curve of her high, firm breast, my nose stopping to inhale the scent of her sweet skin. Slowly, her thighs rose around my back, enveloping me in her aroma. It was only as I felt the silk of her skin against my own that I realized that I was also nude.

Her ankles locked around the muscles of my back and my tongue lashed out to taste every exposed inch of her. I became aware of her soft mewls, filling my ears deliciously, driving my lips lower until I was between the shapely legs that I had long admired from a distance.

Had I been a fool to let her evade me this long, or was I acting impulsively? Again, I forced myself to live in the present, to embrace what was happening and forget about the repercussions of such an act. After all, we were man and wife now. We weren't doing anything wrong.

Then why did I feel so guilty?

My tongue delved into the very core of her, and I felt her fingers curl into my hair, her hips arching upward to meet me as she let loose a series of sighs and moans. I could tell I was hitting precisely the right spots, judging by Vivian's inadvertent jerks and cries. My mouth suctioned onto her clit and I lapped at the succulent nectar of her middle. She was already soaked, ready to climax, and with a few long laps of my tongue, I heard her scream out my name once before a gush of heat covered my face.

I wasn't sure how much more I could take pleasuring her when my own member demanded attention. When I was sure I'd wrung every moment of her climax out of her, I pulled myself up to mount her.

Our gazes locked and I saw the faraway, hazy look in her golden-grass irises. She was somewhere else, floating in pleasure.

"I haven't even started with you," I promised her, positioning myself between her sopping legs.

With a grunt, I entered her, sliding in seamlessly. I did not expect the tightness that welcomed me, grasping my shaft firmly. A groan escaped me that felt like it was ripped from my gut.

She was so tight, like a virgin, and for a startling second, I wondered if she was one.

The expression of shock on her face told me that she had not been prepared for my size. The gentleman in me warned me to slow my pace, but the beast had already taken over. She was mine now, and I wasn't going to let her forget it—no matter how loud she screamed for mercy.

And she did scream. Her moan of passion intertwined with mewls of pleading as my thrusts grew harder.

I sat back, my fingers tweaking her rigid nipples, determined to take her over the edge again. She writhed underneath me, and with once final pinch, her inner walls clenched tighter around me with urgency.

"I'm going to cum again," she gasped, and no sooner had the words left her rosebud mouth than I felt the flow of juices against my pulsating shaft.

I closed my eyes, willing myself to hold back, but it was already too late for that. My sac had become hard, pulling up tight against my body, and I was about to blow. There was no more willpower. She had brought me to the point of no return.

I exploded inside her, filling her with my seed. I was almost surprised that she didn't jump in pain, because it felt like hot lava was pouring from me and into her, joining us together in final unity.

Vivian's entire body was convulsing, and I lowered my body to press against hers, murmuring softly in her ear. A hand reached up to stroke her blonde hair and to wipe the beads of sweat from her forehead.

"It's all right," I told her, shuddering as the last of my orgasm escaped me. "Just relax."

Slowly, my words seemed to have their desired effect and she stopped shaking as violently. Her breaths slowed and she seemed to melt into me fully. It took me a couple minutes to realize I was probably crushing her under my weight, but Vivian didn't seem to be complaining.

In fact, she hadn't uttered a word in minutes.

"Are you okay?" I asked, pulling back in concern. To my relief, I saw her eyes were still open as she nodded, grinning shakily.

"I'm okay," she laughed. "Better than okay. Are you?"

I nodded, gently falling out of her and rolling over. I saw a flash of disappointment in her eyes as our bodies parted.

I lay on my back, watching her in my peripheral vision.

Suddenly, all the doubts that I'd pushed aside dumped on me like a landslide. Why the hell had I done that?

It was obvious by Vivian's face that she had no such worries. In fact, she was looking at me like she was enamored with me. How hadn't I seen it before? Had I just trapped myself into a marriage with a woman who genuinely cared about me?

The idea sent chills down my back.

"I should probably get back downstairs before Lena gets back," Vivian said, and I could hear by her tone that she wanted me to protest. I couldn't bring myself to do it.

Was I attracted to her? Absolutely.

Did that mean I would have married her if we hadn't found ourselves in a situation where she was about to be deported? Definitely not.

After Kate, the idea of marrying anyone for romantic reasons had not entered my mind, not once. I would never introduce another woman into Lena's life after what my ex-wife had done to her.

But Viv is already in Lena's life. And we're already married, a small voice called out to remind me.

That didn't change the fact that I wasn't in love with her, no matter what my libido had felt in that moment of weakness.

"Yes," I agreed, sitting up abruptly. "You probably should. We wouldn't want her to see us like this."

Vivian's brow knit and she parted her lips, as if she was going to say something. She seemed to think better of it and clamped them closed again. Stiffly, she nodded and moved to find her discarded clothes, carefully shielding her nudity from me. I was embarrassed for both of us, and I hated myself for giving her false hope.

How could I have been so stupid, so blind?

Maybe I was just so used to women looking at me that I'd dismissed Vivian's adoring gaze, or maybe she'd just hidden them too well for me to pick up on it. Or maybe she was just feeling the afterglow of our romp in the hay a little too strongly.

Whatever the reason, I hadn't noticed. And I was already regretting giving into my impulses, even though I knew somehow that Vivian wouldn't let her emotions get in the way of anything.

Or at least that was my hope.

This can never happen again.

Vivian was coldly quiet as she managed to slip her tracksuit back on. I searched for something lighthearted to say but I was saved from having to say anything at all when my cell phone chimed.

It took me a minute to find it in my pants, which were in the sitting room, and by the time I dug it out and looked up, Vivian had left my suite.

Shit.

I was going to have to make nice with her—in a way that didn't involve sex but still kept the peace. It was Christmas, after all, and the last thing I wanted was tension hanging over us over the holidays.

I picked up the phone and saw it was a text from Colin, the resident handyman.

There's someone at the gate for you, Mr. Holloway.

I idly wondered where Krista was, but it didn't really matter.

Who is it?

I watched the iPhone bubbles appear as he responded, and when the message came through, my blood turned to ice.

Someone from the Immigration Department.

I bolted from the bedroom, not bothering to reply to Colin's text, and yelled out for Vivian.

Shit! How can they be here already? It's so close to Christmas, and they're government workers!

"Vivian!" I called through the halls. "Where the hell are you?"

I stopped at the overlook above the foyer and my question was answered. The nanny stood in front of the door. She seemed so small, standing down there before the two official-looking government employees framing the open threshold.

I swallowed the feeling of apprehension filling my windpipe and hurried down the stairs toward her, consciously aware of the fact that my pants were slipping over my hips. Hastily, I did up my belt and ran my hand through the haphazard mess of unruly dark curls on my head.

I knew I looked terrible, but I realized it might work to my advantage.

"Honey!" I called with too much force. "I've been looking everywhere for you!"

Slowly, Vivian turned to look at me, the hurt in her eyes still apparent, but she forced a wan smile.

"Here I am, sweetheart," she sighed. "May I present the Department of Immigration?"

A woman stepped forward, a no-nonsense look about her and I knew she was going to be a bitch. They say not to judge a book by its cover, but it was difficult not to when the pinched expression on her face already told me she hated us. It would be hard to get her to believe a word that came out of our mouths.

"Agent Blair," she introduced, without breaking a smile. "And that's Agent Brody. USCIS."

Her partner didn't seem any more amused than Agent Blair did, and I asked myself if being humorless was a prerequisite for government employees. I'd yet to meet anyone in any branch who had a quick wit.

Looks like our caseworkers won't be any different.

She flashed identification, just in case we thought she might be lying, and I gestured for her to enter.

"Come in," I said genially. "Can I offer you something to drink?"

A smirk formed on Agent Blair's mouth and she shook her head, glancing around the massive foyer. I could read the contempt on her face as I drew closer to Vivian.

All my previous thoughts about keeping my distance were forgotten, and I circled my arm around her waist protectively, hoping we looked like a happy couple. But even as I did it, I could feel the tension radiating off my wife.

She did not have a good poker face.

"Nice place," Agent Blair commented. I noticed that they still hadn't closed the door, and I wondered if that was some kind of power move.

"Thank you. We like it, don't we, hon?" I nuzzled Vivian's neck with my nose, but it was like snuggling a brick wall.

"Why don't we cut the crap, Mr. Holloway?" Agent Brody offered, speaking for the first time, and I looked at him in surprise.

"Pardon me?" I asked, my back tensing. We weren't even going to pretend, I saw.

"We know you married Miss Isaac to keep her in the country. You can cut the act."

My infamous temper flared, but wisely, I hid it beneath a sardonic smile of my own.

"Mrs. Holloway, you mean?" I asked innocently. "Isaac is her maiden name."

Vivian seemed to relax against me just a little, and I felt empowered by her ease. If we stuck together, they couldn't shake us, no matter how hard they tried. I'd certainly been up against worse than these two embittered and likely underpaid souls. But had Viv?

"I didn't realize she had legally changed her name," Agent Blair commented. "Considering you only got married two days ago."

I offered her a phony grin and sighed.

"I suppose she's been Mrs. Holloway to me since the minute we decided to marry," I demurred, channeling my high school acting experience. "If you've ever been in love, you'll understand."

"And when was it that you decided to marry, exactly?" Agent Brody piped in, following his cue. I had to wonder if they didn't rehearse their visits like a choreographed dance. It was certainly working out like one.

"Around the time that Miss Isaac realized she was being deported back to Canada?" he continued, his eyes narrowed with anger. I held my smile. I wished I could see Vivian's face, but I didn't want to risk looking at her dead on. I didn't want to give them the sense that we were exchanging hidden looks at their expense.

Appearances are everything, I reminded myself. *No matter what line of work you're in. If we show them that we at least like one another, they'll probably back off. Cory is working on the paperwork as we speak.*

"Well, that would be defrauding the American government," I replied. "And as you probably know, I have a solid reputation as CEO of Marker-Bynes Inc."

"We know who you are, Mr. Holloway," Agent Blair spat. "We know so many men like you who think they can buy their way out of anything and do whatever the hell they want. But when we prove what you two have done, you will be facing criminal charges."

I stared at her, feeling my pulse quicken, but my gaze didn't falter. Not even when I felt Vivian swallow a gasp.

"You're wrong," I told her evenly, sparks flying from my eyes. "And you know why?"

Agent Blair took the bait.

"Why?"

"Because there are no men like me, Agent Blair. You'll do well to remember that."

7

CHAPTER SEVEN

ivian

LUKE DIDN'T SEEM concerned in the least by our visit from Agents Blair and Brody. I didn't understand how he could be so calm, but I didn't ask him.

No, after Immigration left, I made myself as scarce as possible. I didn't want to be alone with him again, not when he had made his intentions clear after our encounter without even having to say a word.

I tried not to be angry about it, even though he had instigated the whole encounter. I had wanted it as much as he had, but I guess I'd thought it meant more than it did. I had wanted it to mean more than it did.

It was a hard hand to be dealt when a part of me had been sure I could eventually win Luke over. I felt a connection between us that I thought was worth something, even in the middle of the unconventional relationship we'd formed.

But he didn't seem to want that. He wanted a nanny for his daughter, not a wife, and that was the only reason I wasn't back in Canada. I would do well to never forget that again.

I stayed close to Lena for the next couple days. When I wasn't with her, I hid out in my bedroom, not wanting to risk running into Luke, who was planning on staying home until the day after Boxing Day.

It was Christmas Eve and I sat on my bed, surrounded by the colorfully wrapped presents I'd gotten for Lena.

There was one for Luke, too, one I'd bought before all the craziness of Vegas. I stared at the star-laden paper and debated whether to put it under the tree that night when I was sure the household was asleep.

I didn't want him to think I was being clingy or trying to push the boundaries of the relationship he'd so clearly set with his reaction after we'd slept together. I understood the deal now, and I wasn't going to beg him to love me. I had my pride.

Still, what else could I do with it? It was a limited edition Rolling Stones album, one I knew was his favorite.

I had heard him listening to the band many nights, the music fluttering out of his study as he worked into the wee hours of the morning. When I'd found it at the flea market in Salem, I couldn't resist picking it up. At the time, it had only been an innocent gesture from an employee to her boss, but now ...

I sighed and placed it on the pile with the other gifts. There were also small gifts for Krista, Colin, and Burt, as well as for the part-time maids. But again, I was plagued by the thought that maybe they would think I was trying to buy their affections in the aftermath of marrying Luke.

How had my life gotten so complicated in less than a week?

And it was only going to get worse, I knew. Those USCIS agents already loathed us—there was no doubt about that. True, Luke had handled himself with his usual Holloway assuredness, but that didn't mean he wasn't regretting his actions. The threat that charges would be laid had worried me terribly, but I hadn't spoken to him about it.

I didn't want to speak to him about anything, even though I knew I couldn't avoid him forever. Tomorrow we would all be sitting around the tree, opening presents, and our gazes would meet once or twice.

There was a knock on my door and I started, looking around desperately for a place to stash the gifts before anyone saw them.

"Viv, are you in there?"

My eyes widened with surprise. For a minute, I thought about ignoring him, but I realized how childish that would be.

"Yes, I'm here. Give me a second."

I stuffed the pile of presents in the closet and turned to look at myself in the mirror, drawing my hand through my hair.

I rolled my eyes, disgusted with myself for still wanting to look good for him.

"Hey," I said, throwing open the door. "What's up?"

He stared at me sheepishly.

"I ran out of wrapping paper," he confessed. "And Krista says she's out too. I'm sorry to bother you when I know you've been trying very hard to avoid me the past few days."

I felt instantly indignant, and I could feel my eyes narrow at him.

"I have not!" I lied through my teeth.

He grinned. "All right. If you say so."

Our eyes met and I flushed before looking away.

"I have some wrapping paper," I mumbled, turning to find it. I realized it was in the closet and I cast him a look.

"Turn around. I don't want you to see the presents."

I know it sounded ridiculous, like some childish superstition, but it was too late to take it back. Thankfully he didn't laugh at me, but instead turned his broad shoulders away from me. Instantly, I envisioned my nails digging into the muscles of his back.

My blush deepened and I was grateful that he wasn't looking at me, but it took me a minute to compose myself.

"Here. It's not much, but I assume you don't have that much to wrap."

I tossed him the half-empty roll of wrapping paper and he

thanked me. We stared at one another awkwardly for a few seconds before I looked away.

"Viv, I ..."

"It's fine," I said quickly. "We don't have to talk about it. I get it."

And I really did—but that didn't make it hurt any less.

"It's not that I don't care about you," he explained, somehow adding insult to injury. "I love how you are with Lena, and I know this house has been so much better with you in it. That means more to me than I can tell you. It's just ..."

Again, he trailed off, and I felt a flash of annoyance course through me. I didn't need to be handled. I knew what I had walked into—he didn't have to tell me that he didn't love me.

"Luke, I'm telling you, I get it. As soon as the investigation is over and a reasonable amount of time has passed, we'll divorce as we discussed. You don't have to worry."

"I'm not worried," he replied gruffly. "I'm trying to explain to you that I do care about you, just not in the way you want."

I bristled, my make-no-waves personality evaporating, and I glared at him defiantly. "What the hell do you know about what I want?" I snapped. "You don't know a damned thing about me!"

My about-face left him visibly startled and he held up his hands.

"I don't claim to know what's in your head, Vivian," he backpedaled, but it didn't matter. I was already feeling humiliated. He knew that I was in love with him, somehow, and he was patting me on the head like a puppy and giving me a bone to placate me.

If I hadn't loved Lena as much as I did, I would have packed my bags right then and stormed out of the house. I deserved to be treated better than that. I wasn't just his daughter's nanny, not anymore.

But, of course, I didn't leave. Even if I'd had somewhere to go, I was married to him now, and I would be damned if Lena would wake up on Christmas morning to learn that another mother had left her.

I steeled my temper and tried to stuff down all the words that threatened to spring from my lips.

"That's right," I said after I'd collected myself somewhat. "You don't know what's happening in my head. I'm fine with everything the way it is. I'm your wife on paper for Lena's benefit, but there's nothing between us. Nor would I want there to be. What happened the other day was a one-time thing. To make the marriage official, I guess."

I don't know how I managed to say the words without my voice cracking, but somehow I managed. I couldn't keep a little bit of bitterness from seeping into the last sentence though. I still couldn't wrap my head around what he had been thinking the other day, initiating things between us. I knew what I had been thinking—I'd always wanted him—but what was his deal?

Maybe he was one of those guys who fantasized about sleeping with the nanny, and our sham marriage just gave him his best opportunity. That didn't feel right, though.

Luke exhaled slowly and nodded, not meeting my eyes.

"Okay. Then we have an understanding," he said quietly. Was it my imagination or did he sound sad?

Probably my imagination.

"I'll see you in the morning," he said, moving toward the door. I wanted to call out to him, to ask him why he couldn't love me, ask him whether he truly felt no connection between us, but I managed to keep my tongue in my mouth.

"Sure," I replied dully.

He stopped and turned back to me, his green eyes alight.

"Merry Christmas, Viv."

Again with the "Viv." Did he know how much he was torturing me?

"Merry Christmas, Luke."

He left me alone in the bedroom and a sense of great loss washed over me as soon as he was gone. It was in the open now, our business marriage. Whatever we had shared in those moments of passion had been just that—fleeting moments of passion. I was going to have to learn to accept that, even if it broke my heart.

. . .

THE FOLLOWING MORNING, I was up even before the house staff. Well, I hadn't really slept, so there was that.

I made my way into the living room, pausing to behold the beauty of it. Two trees, adorned top to bottom with glass balls and snow-capped decorations, stood by a huge window. Both were overflowing at the base with presents. When I had added mine to the pile the previous night before falling into a fitful sleep, there had been half as many gifts as there were at that moment. Someone else had come in and added to the mass, and I wondered if it had been Luke. The idea that he might have been wandering the mansion sleeplessly at the same time I had been struggling to rest my mind gave me a sense of solidarity. I was glad I wasn't alone in my discomfort, twisted as that sounded.

I was surprised to find Lena awake not long after I was up. She flew into the giant living room, as excited as I'd ever seen her. I had already lit the fire, and outside it looked like another snow had fallen overnight.

"MERRY CHRISTMAS, VIV!" she screamed, throwing herself into my arms.

"Merry Christmas!" I laughed, reeling backward at the impact. It was hard to hold onto my bad mood when her excitement was so infectious.

"Where is everyone?" Lena demanded. "Don't they know it's Christmas?"

"Their minds know it, but their bodies are telling them it's six o'clock in the morning," I replied dryly. "Let them sleep in a bit."

Lena pouted, still somehow managing to look adorably happy.

"Can I open my presents?"

I was at a loss. I had no idea how they did things on Christmas morning in this house, but I had a feeling gift opening without Dad was frowned upon.

"Why don't we wait until your dad wakes up?" I suggested. "Can I make you a hot chocolate?"

Her eyes glimmered.

"Yes, please! Daddy usually makes me one every Christmas morning too!"

I had not known that, but I was glad I was following some semblance of normalcy.

"Want to keep me company in the kitchen?" I didn't want to leave the curious six-year-old alone with that freakish mound of presents. I wasn't sure any child should have to endure that level of self-control.

"Viv, why don't you and Daddy sleep in the same bed?"

I almost stopped mid-step but managed to continue without missing a step.

"Well, we're still getting to know one another," I started. It was not a question I'd prepared for. How did this kid know so much about adult relationships? Had Luke had a live-in girlfriend before?

The idea of another woman being in Luke's life before me gave me a jolt of unexpected jealousy, even though I knew, rationally, I was being ridiculous. Of course he'd had other women in his life. He hadn't become a priest just because his wife had left.

It had just never occurred to me before that moment.

"Shouldn't you know someone before you marry them? That's what Daddy always says."

"You talk to your dad about marriage?" I asked, somewhat surprised. That was a big conversation for a little girl.

"Kind of. He always says that he didn't know my mom as well as he should have before he married her and they had me."

Tears sprang into my eyes and I quickly blinked them away, her words a little too on the nose. Even though we'd known what we were doing when we'd agreed to this crazy marriage, I couldn't help but feel that Luke would be as regretful about his second marriage as he was his first.

"Then he tells me to make sure I know someone inside and out before I decide to get married."

I inhaled, turning my back to her so she wouldn't see the stricken look on my face. I stepped inside the pantry to find the hot chocolate, but I could still hear her little voice talking.

"So shouldn't you have known Daddy really well before you married him?"

I inhaled deeply and exited the cupboard.

"Your dad and I have one thing in common that is much more important than knowing everything about each other," I explained, setting the tin down on the island where she sat. "And that's you. Your happiness is more important than anything else."

"But you said that you didn't need to be with Daddy to care about me," she reminded me, throwing my earlier words back in my face. I groaned inwardly, wondering how I could possibly explain the situation.

"You ask too many questions for a girl that has a pile of presents waiting to be opened," Luke commented, sauntering into the kitchen.

"Merry Christmas, Daddy!" Lena cried, spinning on the stool to face him. They hugged one another as I moved to start on her hot chocolate.

"Merry Christmas, pumpkin. Are you ready to make a mess?"

He was talking to her but he was looking at me.

"Can I open my presents now?" Lena demanded. "Viv wouldn't let me."

Luke snickered. "That's because you can't pull one over on Viv. Yeah, go in the living room. We'll be there in a minute."

She didn't need to be told a second time, and all I could hear was the echo of her feet slapping against the tiles as she retreated to the living room.

"You don't need to worry about explaining anything to her," Luke told me when Lena was out of earshot. "She'll stop asking questions about us once she adjusts to the idea."

And by that time, we'll be divorced, I thought grimly, but I didn't say it aloud. I was sure he had considered that too.

Instead, I nodded. "I know."

"I have something for you," he continued. From the inside of his robe, he removed an envelope, handing it over to me. My brow furrowed and I exhaled slightly, knowing that I had done the right thing leaving his present under the tree. He had gotten me a present too.

It doesn't mean anything, I told myself, trying very hard to believe it. After our conversation, I knew he hadn't changed his mind about me overnight, but I still couldn't help being hopeful about what the envelope held.

"Go ahead," he urged. "Open it."

Nervously, I obliged, my mind playing out what it could contain. Maybe a gift certificate or tickets somewhere exotic. Or maybe a—

I stopped myself and eyed the piece of paper in my hand. It was a check for five thousand dollars.

I felt hot and cold all at the same time, and I could feel my body starting to tremble. I had bought him a heartfelt present, and he had given me a check.

"It's your Christmas bonus," he explained, smiling proudly. "Just don't tell anyone else how much it is, okay? I don't want the staff getting up in arms about it."

I scoffed, but again tried to stuff down the venom threatening to spill from my lips.

If it hadn't been crystal clear before, it punched me directly in the face now. I was his employee. All that talk about caring for me had been bullshit. I thought about what Agent Blair had said, about Luke paying to get his way, and I wondered if there wasn't some truth to it.

"Thank you," I said stiffly, taking a deep breath and whirling away as the milk began to boil on the stove. "That's very kind."

He was silent for a minute.

"Are you upset? Were you expecting more?"

I laughed and spun back toward him. I could only stare at him, and suddenly I wasn't angry at all, only deeply wounded.

He really didn't see what was wrong here, which led me to wonder if I was the one looking at everything weird.

"Are you guys coming?" Lena yelled. "I'm going to start opening presents soon!"

"Vivian?"

I shook my messy mop of blonde hair, the strands falling into my eyes, and returned to making Lena's hot chocolate.

"Nothing is wrong. I'm just overwhelmed." At least that much was true.

He didn't look convinced, but I was in that moment. I knew where I stood with Luke, and I wouldn't forget it again.

I was only his daughter's nanny, and that was all I would ever be.

8

CHAPTER EIGHT

Luke

I COULD FEEL the tension mounting in the house as the days passed. Even though there was none of the drama that Kate had inspired during our marriage, something was brewing beneath the polite smiles and nods that Vivian and I exchanged when we passed in the halls.

She suddenly wasn't around on her nights off, instead going into the city and arriving home well after I'd gone to bed. I found myself wondering if she'd found a boyfriend, but I knew it wasn't really my place to ask, even if the thought did give me an uncomfortable feeling in the pit of my stomach.

What if the USCIS agents were watching her? They hadn't been back to my house yet, but they were bound to appear or set up an appointment some time.

"I can't do anything about her citizenship while she's under investigation," Cory explained to me when I asked him how long it would take to get her paperwork pushed through. "It might have been better to have had sent her back to Canada and sorted it out there."

"No, it wouldn't have," I growled. "Lena would never have survived it emotionally."

"It sounds like you might not have come out of it too great, either," my lawyer commented dryly.

"Just see what it's going to take to move things along, Cory. How long is this investigation going to last?"

"As long as it lasts. If they want to make your life miserable, they will. Your girl could be in for a long, painful process."

"But they won't send her back while she's married to me, right?"

"I never claimed that," Cory protested. "She's a Canadian citizen. Granted, you have more pull than most, and they probably won't want to piss you off, but they could still send her back at any time, Luke."

The words made my blood run cold.

"How can I make sure she doesn't get sent back? Ever."

"You can't. Unless you hide her somewhere," he chuckled, but I wasn't amused.

The idea played in my mind for a few seconds, and Cory seemed to pick up on my thoughts.

"I was kidding! Are you crazy? You're already committing a federal offense by marrying her for a green card. Do you want to add obstructing a federal investigation to the charges?"

"I'm trying to find a way to keep my wife from being deported," I snapped. "That's why I'm wasting my time talking to you!"

"Your wife? I thought she was Lena's nanny."

"Cory ..." I felt my cheeks burn. "Just do something about this."

"I'll see if I can work my magic."

We disconnected our call and I found myself pacing around my study, glancing at my watch.

It was nine o'clock and Vivian still wasn't home.

As if on cue, I heard the alarm beep as the front door opened. I headed toward the foyer, my blood racing.

"Where the hell have you been?" I barked at her. "Do you know what time it is?"

She blinked at me in surprise.

"It's like nine o'clock," she replied. "Did I wake you?"

"Wake me? I haven't slept in weeks! Vivian, you can't keep disappearing on your days off. What if the USCIS come calling?"

Her look of confusion didn't fall away, but a hint of defiance joined it.

"Am I under house arrest?" she asked, the question sincere.

Her sincerity snapped me out of my fit. Of course she wasn't under house arrest. Why was I overreacting? If the agents showed up and she wasn't home, who cared? It would be their fault for not making an appointment.

"No, you're not," I conceded grudgingly. "But what if they're following you and I'm not with you?"

She simply looked more perplexed. I was beginning to feel like a madman.

"You have to be with me constantly?"

Again, the question was real. She was trying to make sense of my irrational anger, but how could she do that when I wasn't sure why I was so keyed up myself?

"No ..." I inhaled sharply, willing my brain to work normally.

She stalked toward me slowly and I saw diamond-like flakes of snow in her hair, melting away and leaving a shiny crown across her forehead. She might not have liked the cold, but the cold loved her. Her complexion was a healthy, glowing red and her eyes sparkled with unshed tears from the wind. She looked like a frozen angel.

"What's going on?" she asked nervously. "Is something wrong?"

"I don't know," I confessed. "I have a bad feeling something's going to happen and I don't know how to stop it."

"Something like what?" she choked, her face cocked upward to look at me with fear. "I'm getting deported anyway?"

"I don't know," I insisted. "I just get these feelings sometimes, Viv. I know that something's coming."

"Maybe we should call USCIS and see how the investigation is going," she suggested. "Instead of waiting around. It's been three weeks since they were here and we haven't heard anything else. Maybe they've closed the file."

"They haven't," I replied flatly. "I just got off the phone with Cory. He can't move your paperwork along until they're done with their investigation."

She pursed her lips together and continued to study my face through narrowed eyes.

"Then we have to call them. Maybe we can invite them here. Move things along."

I nodded slowly, exhaling slightly. I don't know why I was relieved to hear that we were still on the same page. She'd never indicated that she'd changed her mind, but we hadn't been the closest since Christmas. I was troubled by how much she had pulled away.

I missed the short friendship we'd developed, the mild bantering, and spending time together when I was home. Lena asked about her absence constantly and I never had any idea what to tell her.

"Sorry, honey, your fake step-mom is keeping her distance from me because we slept together and messed everything up" didn't quite have the right ring to it.

"Vivian is out living her life," was the best I could come up with, but it proved to be the wrong thing to say.

"I thought we were her life," my daughter muttered, and I felt like a jackass. The last thing I wanted was to turn Lena against Vivian.

"You'll understand when you get older," I concluded, using the cop-out conversation-ender that only parents could use.

"Luke, we'll have to be more convincing when they come again. Show more unity in the home," she murmured.

I eyed her speculatively. "What do you mean?"

"We, uh ..." she stopped speaking, presumably to get the words out properly. "We should have a bedroom together, in case they want to look."

Her blush was deep but she held my gaze unflinchingly. There was something different about her, and I was only noticing it for the first time. She didn't look at me the same as she had before.

It bothered the shit out of me.

"You're right," I agreed. "I should have thought about that before. You can move your stuff into my suite tonight."

Her brow knit and she shook her head.

"I'm not really moving into your suite," she explained. "I'm just suggesting we make it look like we share a bedroom."

"Oh."

I was confused at the overwhelming sense of disappointment her words caused. I couldn't get a handle on my conflicting emotions—a mess of hot and cold, of wanting to press my mouth to hers and wanting to wrap her in my arms and thank her for being able to move past hating me.

Her gaze remained on me and it felt like a dare, a challenge, somehow. I was up for it.

I reached for her, pulling her toward me and crushing my lips downward. She gasped in shock and instantly yanked herself back.

"What the hell are you doing?" she choked, wiping my kiss from her mouth with the back of her hand. "Are you crazy?"

I thought over that question very seriously. I must have been crazy to pull something like that, and she had every right be as furious as she was.

"I'm sorry," I sighed. "I couldn't help myself."

"I think that's just the damned problem, Luke, you always help yourself," she whipped back at me.

"What's that supposed to mean?" I demanded. I knew she was upset, and rightfully so, but she didn't need to dig at my character like that.

"Never mind," she snapped, whirling toward the stairs. "I'm going to bed."

I watched her storm up toward her bedroom and before I could stop myself, I bolted up after her.

I caught up with her at her bedroom door.

"Don't follow me! I don't want to see you right now!"

There were tears in her eyes and I knew that I had confused her and hurt her with my kiss—bringing up any feelings she'd managed to suppress these past couple weeks. But I couldn't feel guilt about it, not when she'd awakened the beast in me too.

I nudged her back into her bedroom and closed the door, my own eyes flashing.

"You think I take what I want?" I demanded furiously. "I've worked my ass off my entire life to get where I am. Everything I do, I do for my daughter."

Her face did not soften.

"Yeah, like having your way with me and then announcing you have no feelings for me. That helps Lena a lot," she spat back. It was a slap in the face and for a moment, I was speechless.

"Vivian, that day—"

"Oh just spare me! I'm here for Lena too—really here for her. If it wasn't for her, do you think I'd put up with your hot and cold crap? I'm her nanny, I'm not your side chick or booty call or whore or whatever the fuck you think I am! You can't just write me a check and make things go back to normal again."

I had never heard her swear before, and I hated to admit it, but it turned me on. I wanted to kiss her again, to feel those crude lips on mine—but I didn't risk it. I was liable to get hurt.

"I never thought of you like that," I told her softly, stopping in my tracks. "I could never think of you like that."

"Yeah," she snorted. "That's why you just tried to stick your tongue down my throat again."

"Vivian, I care about you—"

If she'd had something in her hand, I was sure she would have whipped it at my head, and the look she gave me was enough to shut me up.

"Get. Out."

I didn't want to leave. I wanted to stay there and talk her down and make her see that I wasn't the rich, entitled asshole she was beginning to see me as. I wanted my friend back, my companion, but there was no way I could achieve that, not when I felt like I was melting under her furious gaze.

"All right," I muttered, turning back toward the hallway. "I'll go."

I crossed the threshold, determined to say something that might resonate with her, but the door slammed inches from my nose and the noise reverberated through the halls.

"Daddy?"

Ah shit.

"Hey, honey. What are you doing up?"

"I heard yelling. Are you and Viv fighting?"

"No, no," I lied, hurrying toward her and steering her back toward her bedroom. "You must have had a bad dream."

"I was awake."

There really was no arguing with any of the women in my life.

"I have no idea what you heard," I fibbed again. When you first become a parent, you swear you'll never lie to your kid. Full disclosure, you say, no room for dishonestly in this house.

But then they grow up ...

"Daddy, is Viv leaving us?"

I felt a stab of worry.

"Why? Did she say something?"

"No, but I think she's not happy here anymore. Was Mommy happy before she left?"

Oh God.

"Vivian is going to stay here as long as possible," I assured her, and I knew in my heart that was true. No matter how angry Vivian was with me, she loved Lena far too much to leave her.

"What do you mean as long as possible? Why wouldn't it be possible for her to stay?"

"Lena, she's not going anywhere, okay?"

My daughter stopped walking as we reached her suite and stared at me with eyes so much like my own.

"I don't believe you."

My brows almost hit my hairline.

"What?"

"I don't believe you, Daddy. I think she's leaving and that's why you were fighting." She was starting to sound a little frantic, and I'd be lying if I said I didn't feel that way too.

"No," I told her, crouching to her level. "Look at me, Lena. I will do everything in my power to make sure that Vivian stays with us."

She cocked her head and studied me speculatively.

"Daddy, do you really love Vivian? Or did you marry her so that I would have a mommy?"

I closed my eyes and opened them again before answering.

"Lena, when you're older, you'll understand that life isn't always so simple. There are so many—"

"So you don't love her."

I gaped slightly and tried to think of a way to talk myself out of this question.

If I say it aloud, it doesn't make it real, I reasoned. *If I say it to placate my daughter, it doesn't make it true.*

Then why was I having such a hard time saying it?

"You shouldn't have married her, Daddy," she frowned at me, the expression reminding me of the other frowning female I'd just left moments ago. "Now Viv is sad all the time."

She didn't give me a chance to respond before disappearing into her room and closing the door in my face. It was the second door I'd had shut on me in five minutes.

I hoped that this wouldn't become a habit.

Slowly, I continued down the hall toward my bedroom. I was suddenly exhausted. My legs were weighted and heavy and my chest felt compressed.

Over and over, Lena's little voice echoed in my mind.

"You shouldn't have married her, Daddy. Now Viv is sad all the time."

It burned so badly in my soul because I knew my daughter was right—I had come up with a terrible plan to keep my daughter happy, and now everyone was paying the price for my poor judgement.

But what's the solution?

I closed my eyes and let myself fall back onto the bed, sinking into the comforter. There was a solution to every problem, I just had to find it.

How could I keep Vivian, Lena, and myself happy?

I fell asleep on the question and woke on the answer—and to someone pounding on my bedroom door.

Before I could register what was happening, Krista burst into my bedroom, her eyes fraught with worry.

"Luke, there are government agents here," she choked. "They're downstairs."

I bolted upright and noticed that dawn had barely broken through the horizon.

"What the hell are they doing here at this hour?" I demanded, rushing after Krista. In seconds, I had my answer as I encountered a group in the hallway. Vivian was flanked between Agents Blair and Brody, handcuffed.

Vivian turned and looked at me, her hazel eyes haunted and terrified.

"What the hell is this?" I yelled at one of the agents. "You can't take her!"

"We have recommended that she be deported back to Canada, Mr. Holloway," Agent Blair said flatly. "We haven't decided whether to press charges against either of you, but we will be in touch."

Dread and indignation filled me and I ran toward them, but I stopped dead in my tracks when I heard Lena's voice call out to me.

"Daddy? Daddy!"

Gooseflesh exploded over my arms and I watched in dismay as Vivian disappeared.

"Daddy! Where are they taking Viv? Is she being arrested?"

"It's okay," I told Lena, pulling her to my side. "It's fine. Everything will be fine."

"No! Daddy, you promised you would do everything to keep her here! Go get her! Don't let them take her!" she sobbed.

Her howls of agony were gut-wrenching, and I wanted so badly to hold her in my arms and cry with my daughter. But I couldn't let myself fall apart.

I had to find a way to bring Vivian home.

9

CHAPTER NINE

ivian

THEY HADN'T ALLOWED me to bring anything with me. When I landed in Vancouver, I was still wearing the clothes I'd been permitted to hastily change into when they'd snatched me out of bed that morning.

Thankfully, I had my purse, and I was still sitting on that five-thousand-dollar check that was supposed to be my "bonus." It had felt tawdry to cash it after what had happened between me and Luke, but now I was back in survival mode, without anywhere to go.

I'd been held in detention until my flight and they hadn't allowed me to call anyone. A part of me had hoped—right up until the second the plane took off—that Luke's lawyer would come smashing through the doors with some injunction or brief or whatever the hell lawyers use to block injustices.

"Stop!" he'd cry. *"You can't remove this woman! She's an American treasure."*

So it wasn't my finest hour, but I was desperate—hoping, praying, pleading silently that I wouldn't be wrenched from the only family I'd ever known.

But there I was, standing in North Van, looking around for a cheap hotel to call home.

It had actually happened. I had been deported, and that meant I could never return to the States again. My step-daughter would have to come visit me in Canada, if her father would arrange it.

Hot tears filled my eyes but I refused to let myself break down, especially not in the crime-ridden neighborhood of North Vancouver, where people were just looking for someone like me to victimize.

As I stood there, looking around for somewhere to go, a rumble of thunder interrupted my thoughts. I looked up as storm clouds circled above my head, forecasting my future.

Home sweet home, I thought bitterly. *I've come full circle.*

"Viv, your order's up!" Ricky called, dinging the bell. "You're taking forever."

I glanced up from the counter and hurried along with my bussing, wondering how the hell people made a career out of waitressing. I'd been working in the diner for three months and it only seemed to get harder, not easier.

Still, living in Vancouver was not cheap, and I was lucky to have a job at all.

"Hello? Earth to Vivian!"

"I'm coming," I told him, moving toward the window. No sooner did I snatch up one plate than three more showed up to replace it.

I inhaled sharply and cast Ricky a baleful look. I believed that he purposely piled up the orders just to watch me run. He flashed me a hideous grin.

"Faster, sweetie. They aren't going to serve themselves." He punctuated his statement with a sleazy wink.

I bit back a scathing response. I needed the job, no matter how despicable the employees and the customers were. It was a truck stop just off the main highway, and while the truckers who came through were always pleasant, the regulars were horrible creatures who had no problem grabbing my ass at will. The owner didn't care, and the waitresses were used to it. Apparently, I was the only one who had any thoughts on the matter.

"Oh, ain't you a sweet thing," an old grandmother cooed at me as I placed her all-day breakfast order before her. It defied logic that she would be able to eat it all, but her companion, a bucktoothed kid of about twenty, dug into his plate with gusto.

"Thank you," I replied, smiling at her. "Is there anything else you need?"

"Look, Stevie. Ain't she pretty?"

The kid barely looked up at me, and I was grateful for that much. I sensed that Grandma was trying to play matchmaker, and that was the last thing I needed.

"How old are you, honey?"

"Twenty-six," I sighed, glancing meaningfully over my shoulder toward the serving window, but Grandma wasn't done.

"You're only a few years older than Stevie, but don't you worry, he'll make a good daddy. He's got two of his own already, ain't that right, Stevie?"

I felt the blood drain from my face and I stared at her.

"What?" I whispered.

She grinned at me knowingly and blinked her rheumy eyes.

"You're pregnant, ain't ya?"

My mouth fell open and I stepped back from the table, wondering if she was some kind of witch.

"I ..."

The old lady howled and slapped the table.

"Did ya see her face, Stevie?" she chortled. "It's all right, honey. Ricky told me all about you. I'm his grandma, too."

I hated Ricky with every fiber of my being in that moment. I didn't justify her words with a response, but simply headed toward the back, my blood boiling.

"How dare you talk my personal business?" I snarled.

Ricky simply smirked at me. "I hate to be the bearer of bad news, sweetie, but there's no such thing as personal business around here."

"Ricky, why would you tell her something like that? I know you don't like me, but this is going too far!"

He shrugged, and for a minute, I saw a flash of humility in his eyes.

"I was just trying to help," he replied nonchalantly and I resisted the urge to reach out and slap his face.

"How the hell is that helping?"

"My grandmother knows everyone. She can set you up and you'll be good."

I blinked at him uncomprehendingly.

"How will I be good?" I demanded, trying to follow his logic, but I knew I was probably wasting my time. His next words, however, sent chills through my body.

"Because, Viv, no one should have to raise a baby alone."

I gaped at him, realizing for the first time that I might actually have a friend in Vancouver, no matter how misguided he might be.

"Now hurry the hell up and serve those dishes."

I WAS thirteen weeks and four days along, but I still hadn't found a way to tell Luke about the baby. I knew I would have to at some point, but in a way, I felt like I was protecting him by keeping it a secret.

Or maybe I was protecting myself. What would he do when he found out? Would he file for divorce and sue for custody? Our divorce was inevitable, but the thought of giving up my baby was unbearable.

I reasoned that he would never be so cruel, that he didn't hate me, no matter how we had left things the night before I was deported.

I'd only spoken to him twice since returning to Canada, and both by accident. I was very careful to plan my calls at a time when I knew Lena would be home from school but that Luke would be at work. Those two times I'd been wrong.

The first time was the day after my deportation.

"Where are you?" he demanded. "We're coming to see you right now."

"No," I told him, trying to keep the emotion from my voice. "You need to stay put and deal with USCIS. For all you know, they're coming back for you next. If you come here, they might think you're fleeing the country."

I didn't know if that was true or not, but it certainly sounded like Agents Blair and Brody had it out for us. I should have foreseen the deportation, but I had gotten too comfortable in my life, too secure in the fact that I could hide behind Luke's name.

No matter how tense he had made me or how many mixed signals he had thrown at me, I really had felt at ease there, comfortable. Stupid.

"I'll talk to Cory. What do you need? I'll send you anything you want."

The desperation in his voice pierced my heart but I knew, even then, that I couldn't take anything else from him.

I wanted nothing more than for him to come to me, to bring Lena so I could comfort her when I knew she was going through hell, but I had to let them go. What other choice did I have? I couldn't be a nanny to Lena while living in Canada.

"Where are you staying?" he demanded.

"It doesn't matter. I think it's best that I don't talk to you again," I said. "I won't be calling again, but I just wanted to say thank you for everything you've done for me. You don't have to worry about me. I'm fine."

"What?" he asked and I could hear the disbelief in his voice. "You're just going to walk away from us like that?"

Bile bubbled in my stomach, but I knew I needed to remain firm. There was no point in drawing out the inevitable. Lena could not move on if she clung to some false hope that we would be reunited. It was unfair to her, no matter how much it broke my heart.

"It's for the best," I told him, my voice cracking.

That had been three months earlier and easier said than done. I couldn't stop myself from calling Lena, and every time I got off the phone, I would hate myself for bringing her to tears when we had to say goodbye.

I missed her desperately. At night, when I couldn't sleep, I would tell my unborn baby about her sister.

"You'll meet her, I promise," I explained. "When I figure out a way to tell your daddy about you. I've already lost your daddy and sister. I can't bear the thought of losing you too."

My usually flat stomach was just starting to swell, and I rubbed the skin gently.

I already loved the peanut growing in my belly, even though the month of morning sickness had almost killed me. It was just a reminder to me that, no matter how bad things got, I would never give up on her, not the way my parents had given up on me.

"It's going to be you and me against the world," I promised as I lay on my dilapidated mattress and stared at the ceiling.

The one-bedroom apartment was a step up from the boarding house I'd landed in after my deportation, but it was still a hellhole.

Look at how far you've come—from an en suite in a mansion to a leaky one-bedroom in a shitty neighborhood.

It would have been so easy for me to call Luke and tell him everything. I was sure he'd have me in a new apartment in two hours, but my pride and sense of independence didn't permit it.

Of course, in the back of my mind lingered the thought that Luke always bought his way into whatever he wanted. He would not buy my child too.

I wondered if I was being unfair, if the fact that I was suffering through unrequited love for the man had altered my perspective of the truth.

Over and over, I thought of the good times we'd had, both before and after the wedding.

We had almost been like a real family once, and now...

My life was bittersweet. I was beside myself some nights, fighting with my own hand as I reached for the phone to call him, and other nights, I was blissfully content to know that I had my baby all to myself.

All I knew for certain was that whatever life I'd had living under the same roof with Luke—good, bad, or indifferent—was over for good.

10

CHAPTER TEN

Luke

LENA DIDN'T LOOK at me the same way anymore. Her sweet, sunny disposition dissipated as soon as Vivian left, and I knew exactly how she felt—my soul felt like it had been ripped from my body too.

That awful morning, I had woken up to the realization that I was in love with Vivian. It was not because of Lena, or some self-serving drive to possess her, but a genuine love that had snuck up on me over the months she'd been in our lives.

But I'd come to the conclusion too late, and now she was gone—ripped out of my life forever.

Lena blamed me, and she was right to, but she couldn't hate me more than I hated myself for what had happened. Even if I'd done everything I could in terms of USCIS, I had not done everything I could for Vivian.

My phone rang and I snatched it up.

"Cory! What have you got?"

"I haven't found her," my lawyer sighed. "But she found you."

I had no idea what that meant.

"Speak English."

"Vivian is filing for divorce."

The words punched me in the face and I physically reeled backward.

"What?" I choked. "How—how do you know?"

"I got the papers at my office," Cory explained. "Do you want me to bring them to you or—"

"I'm on my way."

I hung up and snatched my keys out of my desk drawer. Cory was in Boston, only a few blocks from my offices, and I almost considered running over on foot but I wisely took my car. I needed the head-space to get myself together.

I'd commissioned one of his private investigators to find Vivian. I knew that she was in Vancouver, but it was a big city—a big Canadian city. Whatever resources Cory's PIs had did not extend across the border. My next step was finding one closer to her home.

Even if she didn't accept my declaration of love, I needed to let her know how I felt about her before she dismissed me completely.

I knew Vivian had been calling Lena regularly the last few months. I hadn't been wrong about her—she would never give up on my child. But I was another story. I didn't have high hopes that she would take my words at face value, but all I could do was try.

But I had to find her first.

I arrived at Cory's office in minutes, parking my Jag in the visitor's lot. Under normal circumstances, I would have been thrilled to be riding around in my springtime vehicle, but I had barely noticed the change in cars or seasons.

My mind had been focused on Vivian and how to bring her back to me.

"Here," Cory sighed when I appeared in his offices. His outstretched hand held a manila envelope, which I snatched up and read. To my relief, I saw her return address.

"Why didn't you just tell me there was a return address?" I snapped, furious with him.

Cory grunted. "Because, Luke, she's giving you an out. She's done with this charade and you should be too. There's no reason to keep doing this to yourself."

I understood now—Cory had wanted to lecture me face to face.

"No chance," I replied, whirling back to leave the office. "I'm not signing anything until I see my wife."

She wasn't home when I got there—or if she was, she wasn't answering the door.

I had considered bringing Lena along with me, but I had no idea what to expect of Viv when I saw her. For all I knew, she might punch me right in the face and order me to leave her the hell alone.

Maybe I should have brought Lena with me, I thought wryly, knowing that Vivian would never tear me a new one in front of my daughter. Too late now.

I sat in my rental car for four hours, watching the crumbling low-rise that Viv had given as a return address. For a while, I wondered if it was a decoy or if maybe a friend lived there. She had been adamant about not telling me where she lived. Would she really have given up her address so easily?

I reasoned that it was a legal court document and that she wouldn't have fibbed it. She needed to have everything in order if she wanted to move forward.

Move forward with our divorce.

It was after midnight when I finally saw her, and at first, I didn't recognize her. She was dressed in a pale blue uniform—like a waitress from the fifties—her hair tucked up into a messy chignon.

I realized with some horror that she must've been working in a diner of sorts.

Why hadn't she just told me she needed money? God, why was she so damned stubborn?

I jumped from the car and scurried across the parking lot. She didn't immediately see me and I knew I should slow my gait if I didn't want to scare her, but I couldn't bring myself to do that. Not when she was so close.

I was almost on her when she whirled and looked at me in shock.

"Luke! Wh—what are you doing here?" she panted, and I could see I had terrified her.

"Don't say anything until I'm done talking," I growled, trying unsuccessfully to keep a neutral tone. "And after that, if you want to tell me to go to hell, I'll go and never bother you again."

The pain in her eyes was clear as she shook her head.

"No," she said quietly, looking around. "We can't do this here. Come inside with me."

I suddenly realized how seedy the neighborhood truly was, a fact that had managed to escape my notice somehow despite the hours I had spent in the car.

She was already through the side entrance of her building, mounting the stairwell.

"This is good," I told her and she stopped halfway up, turning to look at me with wide eyes.

"I can't give you a divorce until you know how I really feel about you," I told her flatly. "I made a mistake not telling you before."

"Luke, you're only saying this because you feel guilty or have some misguided need to protect me, but—"

"No! Listen!" I barked, climbing the stairs two at a time to meet her. "You're wrong. I thought the same thing when I started having feelings for you. I dismissed the jealousy I was feeling as a need to keep you protected, and the attraction I had for you as something else, but I've always loved you. How could I not? You're everything I've ever wanted in a partner."

Under the flickering fluorescent lighting, she stared at me, her face contorting into myriad emotions. I could see she was trying to decide whether or not to believe me, but even I could hear that my words radiated sincerity, full of the feeling I had for her.

"Please, Viv, I don't blame you for walking away from me. I know you think it's the best thing for Lena too, and I would agree with you if—"

Her mouth locked on mine and, without skipping a beat, our bodies meshed together. The relief I felt almost knocked the wind from me completely. It was as if I had been holding onto one giant breath for three months.

Our arms wrapped around one another and in seconds I had her pinned against the wall next to the door, her old-style skirt riding up over her thigh as I raised her calf against my hip.

A slow sigh escaped her mouth when I dropped my lips to the dip in her throat. I found my new favorite spot on her neck, sucking on her gently.

“You have no idea how long I’ve wanted to hear you say those words,” Viv murmured. “I dreamt about it almost from the moment I met you.”

“I’ve been a fool,” I whispered, pulling her tightly toward me and driving the bulge of my crotch against her. Even between the material of my pants and her panties, I could feel the burning heat of her soaking through.

She hadn’t given up on me, and I was never giving up on her. I’d never let her go again.

A soft cry fell from her mouth when my fingers slid over the drenched cleft between her legs. She cocked her head to look at me, nodding eagerly.

“Now,” she breathed. “Take me. I’ve waited far too long for you.”

She didn’t need to tell me twice, and I managed to unzip my pants, slipping my rock-hard shaft against her sweetness.

Her whole body heaved upward when I entered her and she moaned loudly. Once more, I was stunned by the suction of her gripping core and I had to steady myself instantly, worried that I might blow before we even got started.

“Fuck me.”

Ah, that filthy mouth did me in. Suddenly I was plunging into her, driving her against the cinderblocks of the stairwell as her screams radiated through the empty levels. If anyone had considered taking the stairs, they most certainly would have changed their mind after listening to Vivian’s hollers.

Each shriek forced me to drive into her harder, my fingers digging into her shapely ass until I had both legs wrapped firmly around mine. I knew her back would be bruised by the time I finished, but I didn't care anymore than she seemed to.

We climaxed together, me spilling into her as she broke into a burning orgasm. We were a sticky, sweaty combination of smoldering desire.

Viv held fast to me as I let her back onto her feet slowly, gently. She winced and I realized that her feet hurt, probably from working God knows how many hours.

"Viv, what are you doing? Why didn't you ask for my help?"

But I already knew the answer—or at least I thought I did.

She straightened her skirt and kept her eyes averted toward the ground, purposely avoiding my gaze.

"Vivian, look at me," I pleaded with her. "Why didn't you ask me for help? Why did you send me divorce papers?"

A grimace touched her lips and she finally met my gaze. I saw a shadow of regret cross her eyes.

"Because there's something I didn't want to tell you," she murmured so low, I barely heard her.

"What didn't you want to tell me?"

She stared at me for a long moment. "How are we going to do this, Luke? Are you going to come visit me every couple weeks? Bring Lena and upset her life?"

I frowned.

"No," I told her. "We are all going to live together—as a family."

She shook her head.

"How? I can't go back to the States now."

"There are other places to live than the US, you know," I replied wryly. "I've heard Canada is nice, but this neighborhood is making me think otherwise."

She ignored my joke and visibly swallowed.

"You mean it?" she choked. "You would uproot your life so that we could all be together?"

"Haven't you heard a word I've said?" I grunted. "I love you,

Vivian. I won't ever let you go. If being together means we need to move, so be it. I don't think Lena will have any complaints."

To my surprise, Viv began to sob, burying her face in my shoulder.

"Viv, what is it? Why are you crying?"

"Because I'm the idiot," she sobbed. "I'm the one who should be groveling to you."

"Viv, it's all right. Your emotions are just on high alert. Everything is going to be fine," I promised her. "Once we get our family back together."

"You're damn right, I'm emotional—I'm pregnant with our child."

I stared at her in shock for a few moments, unsure whether I was properly processing what she'd just said. She stared at me in consternation, clearly worried about what my reaction would be.

My sudden laughter startled us both.

I leaned my head down and kissed her, first on the lips, then on the nose, then the forehead and anywhere else I could reach before settling back on her lips.

"You're not mad?" she asked cautiously, looking at me from under her eyelashes.

I pressed my hand to her stomach, feeling a slight bump that hadn't been there in all the months she'd lived in my home. I realized now that that was exactly what Vivian had made it—a home.

"Not at all," I whispered, smiling down at her. "After seeing you with Lena all these months, I can't lie and say I never thought about what it'd be like, seeing you with your own child."

She smiled shyly, and the light in her eyes took my breath away.

"You know that I love Lena like my own anyways, don't you? I knew that, no matter what happened between us, I'd always make sure that Lena was a part of her brother or sister's life."

Her words pulled at my heart, and the thought of being able to watch both my girls spoil this new baby—our baby—had a pressure burning at the back of my eyes.

"I bet Lena's going to be thrilled," I said, after clearing my throat.

Suddenly another thought hit me, and I smiled. "You know who I bet won't be thrilled?"

She frowned at me, clearly not liking the thought that anyone would be less than thrilled about our progeny. "Who?" she demanded.

"Agents Blair and Brody, and everyone else at USCIS who thought our marriage was a sham," I replied.

Her startled laughter filled the stairwell, and I leaned down and cut it off with a kiss.

THE END.

ABOUT THE AUTHOR

Mrs. Love writes about smart, sexy women and the hot alpha billionaires who love them. She has found her own happily ever after with her dream husband and adorable 6 and 2 year old kids. Currently, Michelle is hard at work on the next book in the series, and trying to stay off the Internet.

"Thank you for supporting an indie author. Anything you can do, whether it be writing a review, or even simply telling a fellow reader that you enjoyed this. Thanks

❀ Created with Vellum

CPSIA information can be obtained
at www.ICGtesting.com
Printed in the USA
BVHW041517220221
600777BV00006B/417

9 781648 088131